"Close the door," he said, sitting down behind the desk.

I did and took the chair across from him.

He moved his lips as though tasting something, and said, "This is a crap job I have for you, I just want to say that up front. It's a crap job, but the money's good and easy and I need someone I can trust."

"I'll just take my regular fee."

He shook his head. "No. I put in for fifty a day. And expenses, of course. This is the picture business, you take as much money as they'll give you."

"Let's leave that," I said. "What's the job?"

He didn't want to tell. Telling me would make it real. At last he slapped his desk and said, "Oh, hell, you've already seen the kind of thing I have to deal with. These movie people live in a different world than guys like you and me."

"That's not what Life magazine says. Haven't you seen? Bogie built his own porch and Garbo sews all her clothes." Knox snorted at that. "Well, they love and hate and die like anyone else, don't they?"

"Sure," he said, "but they do it to the sound of violins, with their faces ten feet tall..."

The Twenty-Year Death:
THE FALLING STAR

by **Ariel S. Winter**

A HARD CASE CRIME NOVEL

A HARD CASE CRIME BOOK
(HCC-108-Y)
First Hard Case Crime edition: July 2014

Published by

Titan Books
A division of Titan Publishing Group Ltd
144 Southwark Street
London SE1 0UP

in collaboration with Winterfall LLC

Print edition ISBN 978-1-78116-794-6
E-book ISBN 978-1-78116-887-5

Design direction by Max Phillips
www.maxphillips.net

Typeset by Swordsmith Productions

The name "Hard Case Crime" and the Hard Case Crime logo
are trademarks of Winterfall LLC. Hard Case Crime books are
selected and edited by Charles Ardai.

Printed in the United States of America

Visit us on the web at www.HardCaseCrime.com

in memoriam R.C. with apologies

THE FALLING STAR

ONE

Merton Stein Productions was twelve square blocks enclosed by a ten-foot brick wall with pointed granite capstones every three yards. There was a lineup of cars at the main gate that backed out into the westbound passing lane of Cabarello Boulevard. Every five minutes or so the line advanced one car length. If you had urgent business you were no doubt instructed to take one of the other entrances. Since I had been directed to this one, I figured my business wasn't urgent.

It was just about noon on a clear day in the middle of July that wasn't too hot if you didn't mind the roof of your mouth feeling like an emery board. I smoked a cigarette and considered taking down the ragtop on my Packard to let in the mid-day sun. It was a question of whether it would be hotter with it closed or with it open. When it was my turn at the guard stand, I still hadn't decided.

A skinny young man in a blue security uniform stepped up to my open window without taking his eyes off of the clipboard in his hands. His face had the narrow lean look of a boy who hadn't yet grown into his manhood. His authority came from playing dress-up, but the costume wasn't fooling anyone, including himself. "Name," he said.

"Dennis Foster," I said. "You need to see proof?"

He looked at me for the first time. "You're not on the list."

"I'm here to see Al Knox."

He looked behind him, then out to the street, and finally settled back on his clipboard. "You're not on the list," he said again.

Before he could decide what to make of me, a voice said, "Get out of there." The kid was pushed aside and suddenly Al Knox was leaning on my door, wearing the same blue uniform, only many sizes larger. There was a metal star pinned to his chest and a patch below it that stated his name and the title Chief of Security. He stuck his hand in my face and I took it as he said, "Dennis. How the hell are you?"

"Covering the rent. How's the private security business?"

"Better than the public one. Give me a second, I'll ride in with you." He backed out of the window, told the skinny kid, "Open the gate, Jerry, this charmer's with me," and then crossed in front of my car in the awkward lope his weight forced on him. He opened the passenger door, grunted as he settled himself, and pulled the door shut. The sour smell of perspiration filled the car. He nodded his head and pointed at the windshield. "Just drive up Main Street here."

Jerry lifted the gate arm and I drove forward onto a two-way drive lined with two-story pink buildings that had open walkways on the second floors. There was a lot of activity on either side of the street, people in suits and people in painters' smocks and people in cavalry uniforms and women in tight, shiny skirts with lipstick that matched their eyes. Three men in coveralls with perfectly sculpted hair worked bucket-brigade-style unloading costumes from a truck. Workers walked in both directions across a circular drive to the commissary. Knox directed me to the third intersection, which had a street sign that said Madison Avenue. Messrs. Young and Rubicam wouldn't have recognized the place. We turned left, drove one block over, past a building the size of an airplane hangar, and made another left onto a boulevard with palm trees in planters down the middle of the street. Here there was a four-story building large enough to be a regional high school. It had an oval drive and two flagpoles out front, one flying Old Glory and the other flying a banner with the Merton Stein crest on it. We drove past the oval and pulled into a spot at the corner of the building beside a row of black-and-white golf carts.

In front of us was a door with wired glass in the top half that had the word "Security" painted on it in fancy black-and-gold letters. I suppose the men who lettered all those title cards in the old days needed something to keep them busy now. To make doubly sure we knew where we were, a sign on a metal arm above the door read "Security Office." Knox started around the car to lead the way when a woman's voice said something that wasn't strictly ladylike. We looked, and three cars over a blonde head bobbed into sight and then vanished again.

Knox pulled up his pants at the waistband as though they might finally decide to go over his belly, and went around to where we had seen the woman's head. I followed. Bent over, arms outstretched, the blonde made a perfect question mark, an effect accentuated by the black sundress she wore, which covered her from a spot just above her breasts to one just above her knees in a single fluid curve. She had on black high-heeled shoes with rhinestone decorative buckles, simple diamond stud earrings and a necklace with five diamonds set in gold across her white chest. In light of the earrings and the necklace, I allowed that the decorative buckles on the shoes might be real diamonds too. What she was bending over was the back seat of a new '41 Cadillac sedan. A pair of legs in wrinkled trousers was hanging out of the car, the man's heels touching the asphalt. She said the surprising word again, followed by "Tommy."

Knox said, "Do you need any help, Miss Merton?"

She straightened up. There was no sign of embarrassment on the sharp face that came into view, just annoyance and frustration. She brushed her hair back out of her face with one hand, and it stayed exactly where she wanted it, in an alluring sheet that just touched her shoulders. "Oh, Al. Can you help me get Tommy into the car again? He's passed out and he's too heavy for me."

Knox started forward and Miss Merton stepped back out of his way. She looked at me, and a smile formed on her face that suggested we shared a private secret. "Hello," she said. I didn't say anything. Her smile deepened. I didn't like that.

Knox wrestled Tommy's legs into the back seat, a process that involved some heavy breathing and maybe a few choice words under his breath too. At last he had the feet stowed in the well behind the driver's seat, and he slammed the door with satisfaction. "There you go, Miss Merton."

She turned to him, and said in a hard voice, "Tommy can't expect that I'll always go around cleaning up after him."

"No, ma'am," Knox said.

Miss Merton looked at me, gifted me with another smile, and then pulled open the door and poured herself into the driver's seat. Knox faced me, shaking his head but not saying anything as the Cadillac's engine caught and started. Only once the car was out of view did he say, under his breath, "Vera Merton. Daniel Merton's daughter. She's always around here getting into some trouble or other. The son doesn't usually even make it this far. He must have found himself caught out last night." He rolled his eyes and shook his head again. "The bosses, yeah?"

"The bosses," I said.

He gave a hearty laugh and slapped me on the back. "I'm telling you. This place is filled with crazies. Come on into my office, I'll fill you in."

TWO

The front room of the security office was a small, air-conditioned, wood-paneled room with a metal office desk on which there were two telephones, a green-shaded lamp, a desk clock, a pen-and-ink set, a calendar blotter, and a message pad. There was a wooden rolling chair behind it, and three orange armchairs along the wall in front of it that had probably served time on one of the movie sets before their upholstery wore thin and they were reassigned here. A middle-aged dark-haired man with a well-managed mustache looked up as we came in and then away as he saw it was Knox, who continued on through a door behind the desk marked "Private." This led to a narrow hallway off of which there were three more rooms. The first was an empty squad room with four desks, two couches, and a blackboard across one whole wall. The second was a kitchenette with a large table in the center and no less than three automatic coffee machines. Knox went into the third room, which was much like the first, only it had Knox's photographs on the wall. There were pictures taken with various movie stars, and pictures taken when he and I had been police, with Knox looking trim in his city uniform, and pictures taken when he was with the DA's office, looking less trim, but much thinner than he was now. "Close the door," he said, sitting down behind the desk.

I did and took the chair across from him.

"Sorry about the kid at the gate. We have a high turnover and it's either old retired cops like me or kids the academy turned away. The old guys can't take the heat in the box, so it goes to the kids. More than half of this job is managing my own staff."

I said I hadn't been bothered.

He nodded and puffed out his upper lip by forcing air into it. Then he moved his lips as though tasting something, and said, "This is a crap job I have for you, I just want to say that up front. It's a crap job, but the money's good and easy and I need someone I can trust."

"I'll just take my regular fee."

He shook his head. "No. I put in for fifty a day. And expenses, of course. This is the picture business, you take as much money as they'll give you."

"Let's leave that," I said. "What's the job?"

He puffed his lips again and rocked in his seat while rubbing one hand back and forth on his blotter as though checking for splinters. He didn't want to tell. Telling me would make it real. At last he slapped his desk and said, "Oh, hell, you've already seen the kind of thing I have to deal with. These movie people live in a different world than guys like you and me."

"That's not what *Life* magazine says. Haven't you seen? Bogie built his own porch and Garbo sews all her clothes." Knox snorted at that. "Well, they love and hate and die like anyone else, don't they?"

"Sure, but they do it to the sound of violins, with their faces ten feet tall." He slapped his desk again. "If you have any sense of propriety left after being on the force, they sure knock it right out of you here. What do you know about Chloë Rose?"

"I've seen her pictures," I said.

"Well she manages that tortured beauty act from her pictures all the time in real life, too. And now we think maybe she's going crazy."

"What's she done?"

"Nothing much. Nothing besides the usual crying jags and mad demands and refusal to work that we get from any number of these women stars, including some who make the studio a lot less money than Chloë Rose. But now she thinks she's being followed. She's nervous all the time about it, and it's making it hard for Sturgeon to shoot the picture she's making. The studio has her on a five-year contract and there are three years to go, so there are people who are worried."

"Worried that she's actually being followed or worried that she thinks she's being followed?"

"Thinks." He drummed his fingers on the desk. "Maybe she is being followed, I don't know. But I tend to doubt it. These people are all paranoid. It's their sense of self-importance. Either way, I've managed to convince her well enough that I've got things under control here, that the only people on the lot are people who belong there. In truth, there's any number of ways to get onto the lot without us knowing. We have to throw people off the lot all the time, people who think they belong in pictures and are ready to prove it."

"So what do you want me to do?"

"Just follow her around when she's not on the set. Stakeout in front of her house at night."

"You want a bodyguard. I'm not a bodyguard."

"It's not a bodyguard job. I told you, she only thinks she's being followed. You just need to make her feel safe. For show."

"So I'm supposed to follow her around to make her feel better about somebody following her around?"

Knox held his hands wide and leaned back. "That's show business."

"Go back to Miss Rose's mystery man. It is a man, isn't it?"

"That's what she says."

"You said that you convinced her that the only people on the lot are people who belong on the lot. Why couldn't her tail be someone who belongs on the lot?"

"He could be. But don't point that out to her. She must not have thought of it."

"What's he supposed to look like?"

"Like every other man you've ever met, if you go by her description. Medium height, dark hair, medium build. You'll talk to her about it. She'll fill you in."

"And she's seen him on the lot?"

"On the lot and off." He leaned forward. "That's if you believe her. I told you already. There's nobody following her. She's going dotty. There've been a batch of tantrums on the set. And her private life is worse than a paperback novel."

I raised an eyebrow.

He took a breath and let it out slowly. I waited.

"Her husband's Shem Rosenkrantz," he said. "He had a few books they liked in New York ten, fifteen years ago, but the last few years he's been hanging around here doing treatments that never get made. They never get made because he's too busy fooling around with the starlets and he doesn't keep it a secret from his wife. This picture they're filming now is one he wrote and it's getting made because she's in it. And he's *still* having an affair with her co-star, this new girl called Mandy Ehrhardt. Meanwhile, Sturgeon, the director, has a thing for Rose, Missus Rosenkrantz if you're keeping score. Which might be fine if she wanted it too, but…"

"You sure he's not involved with this business?"

"Sturgeon? No. Sturgeon's on good behavior. And he's got reason to be. He had his last three productions fall apart in the middle of filming, and if he doesn't prove he can finish something, he's washed up here."

I mulled it over. "That all?"

"It's not enough?"

"Any old boyfriends that might be tailing her around?"

Knox said through his teeth, "Nobody's tailing her."

"Just for argument's sake."

Knox burst out laughing. "You haven't changed a bit. Still treat every job like it's a real case."

"What am I supposed to do when someone's paying me?"

"This is the picture business, boy. We all get paid for make-believe."

"Silly me," I said. "Always trying to do the right thing."

"You didn't learn anything when they threw you out of the department?"

"Sure, I learned that the law's something they print in books."

He held up his hands, palms out. "All right, all right. I'm not asking you to do anything that'll compromise your precious sense of ethics. All I want is for you to sit down with our star, get her to tell you her story, make lots of notes, and then tell her she doesn't need to worry. And then you can go get drunk in your car or sleep for all I care. It's just for a few days until the picture is done."

"I don't like it. I don't like that what you need's a body-guard, but what you went and got is me. I don't like a job that's not really a job, looking for a man that may or may not exist just to make some actress feel better. Send her to a doctor."

His face turned stormy. "I've already laid out our dirty laundry," he said, and opened his hands over his desk as though it were actually laid out there before us. "More than I ought to have said."

"You didn't tell me anything I couldn't have learned in a movie magazine."

"Come on, Foster. What's wrong with you? This is easy money. I was scratching your back. You got so much work you can turn down fifty dollars a day? Since when?"

"I didn't say I wouldn't do it, I just said I didn't like it."

I could see the muscles of his face relax. He smiled and nodded. He had to be careful, Knox. The littlest thing would give him a coronary someday.

He stood up, his chair rolling backwards as it was freed from his weight. "I did tell you a few things they don't have in the glossies. And I'm sure you'll find out others. If I didn't know how discreet you are…"

And Knox did know. Back on the force, he would have lost his job more than once if it hadn't been for how discreet I was.

"Come on," he said, "let's go meet your client."

I stood too, but waited for Knox to come around the desk. "You're my client, Al."

He opened the door. "At least pretend that you're excited to meet a movie star."

THREE

The first time I saw her in person, it was at a distance and she was on a horse. From what I could make out, she had a small frame; like she weighed less than the saddle they had under her. They had her dressed in a tan leather jerkin with tassels over a blue gingham dress that made no effort to hide a pair of black maryjanes, which I assumed they would keep safely out of the shot. Much of the thick dark hair she was known for was hidden under a ten-gallon cowboy hat. She sat sidesaddle but held the reins like someone who was used to riding the conventional way. Her famous face could have been any pretty girl's at that distance, just a canvas the makeup artist had painted on. Up close I knew she'd look the way I'd seen her dozens of times on posters and billboards and at the pictures. She wasn't a woman, she was a star. Chloë Rose.

We parked the golf cart on the suburban side of the backlot street and walked over to the Old West. The standing set had been built on a stretch of dirt road not quite as long as a football field. There was a ragtag of wooden building fronts lining the street. Some had gotten paint and some hadn't. Each building had a sign, to indicate which one was the saloon, which one was the chemist's, and which one was the jail. It wasn't a bad façade if you closed your eyes and used your imagination.

There were at least fifteen other people on the set—a horse handler, the director, the assistant director, makeup, electric, and some I couldn't identify. As we approached, another woman in a cowgirl costume and a man in a rumpled suit shouted at each other in the shade of the dry goods store. A child of eleven or twelve stood nearby, uninterested.

"You'd better not forget yourself," the man said, "or who got you where you are."

"A washed-up drunk who lives off his wife?"

"You're living off my wife too, aren't you?" That made him Shem Rosenkrantz. "We're all living off of Clotilde on this damn set. I'm just asking for a little favor, that you watch him for a few hours. I've got to work."

She shot her fists out behind her. "Mandy, do this. Mandy, do that. I've paid you back plenty already. Or are you dissatisfied with the service?"

At that, Chloë Rose jerked her horse away from the handler, almost knocking the director over, and cantered to where the couple was fighting. They stopped and looked up at her. The young boy took a step back. "Can't you at least pretend here?" she said in that famous French accent.

Rosenkrantz said something in reply, but Chloë Rose had already turned her horse and brought it almost to a gallop, not slowing until she reached the far end of the Old West set. Rosenkrantz chased after her, running through the cloud of dust her horse had kicked up. As he passed Sturgeon, the director gave him an angry look that was a step away from tears. Rosenkrantz made a placating motion with his hands, still hurrying through his wife's wake.

Knox turned to me. "Wait here. This might not be a good time."

"What makes you think that?" I said.

He started over to the assistant director, who had turned to say something to the director of photography, shaking his head.

I stood with the woman and the kid. She had auburn hair in waves that were too regular to be natural. Her face was angular, so that it was pretty from the front but not as much from the side. When it was angry, which it was just then, all the lines in her face turned sinewy, like she was stretched too tight and might snap at any moment. Knox had warned me off of asking questions, but it was an old habit with me. I said, "Miss Ehrhardt? I'm Dennis Foster. I'm looking into some reports of unusual activity on the set. You see any strange men about? Anyone who doesn't belong? Or maybe he belongs, but not quite as much as he's around."

She didn't turn to look at me while I said all this. She kept her hip cocked with one fist planted on it to show that she was angry. "With all these people around, who knows who any of them are?"

"So you didn't notice anything?"

"Look around. Notice anything you'd like. I'm working."

"I can see that."

She looked at me then. "Was that a crack? You forgot to tell me when to laugh."

"Now would do fine."

She sneered. "Watch it, mister, or I might have to call security."

I pointed to Al Knox, who was making large gestures as he talked, but seemed unable to distract the assistant director from his clipboard. "That's the head of security there. I came with him. Or didn't you notice?"

"I didn't care."

"You don't notice anyone, do you?"

"Sure, today there's been the mailman, the milkman, the ice-man, the priest, a guy from the paper, and a talking cow."

The boy beside her gave one short pant of amusement.

I looked at him, then back at her. "I get it," I said. "You didn't notice anything you feel like talking about. Or at least talking about with me."

"You get paid for being so smart?"

"Not enough."

"What's this all about anyway? Is it because of Chloë?"

I said nothing.

"Chloë's scared of her own shadow. Look at all the time we're wasting now because something upset her fragile disposition."

"I wonder what it could have been."

"You know what? —— Chloë, and —— you too."

"There are children present," I said.

She crossed her arms over her breasts and turned her back to me. I noticed the kid staring at me. I smiled at him, but his face remained impassive. "You see any strange men around?" I said to him.

"I see you," he said.

I nodded. I'd asked for that. I looked around for Knox.

He was on his way back towards me. When he saw me looking he shook his head, his lips pressed together, and waved me over with a swat of his hand. "No dice. They're going to keep shooting now. Sturgeon's only got the horse for another two hours."

I fell in beside him. "I'll meet her later."

"I just would have liked to introduce you," he said. "Smooth your way in."

"I'll manage," I said. We were at the golf cart now.

He stepped up on the driver's side. "Just remember, be discreet," he said, and grunted as he pulled himself under the wheel. "We're keeping this whole thing on the Q.T."

"Mandy seemed to know about it. Says Chloë's paranoid."

"What were you talking to Mandy for? Didn't I tell you not to ask questions?"

I ignored that. "The kid goes with Rosenkrantz?" I said.

"Yeah. By his first wife, I guess. Visiting from back east."

"And how does Chloë feel about that?"

He began to answer but someone cried, "Quiet!" and he fell silent. He gestured for me to do the same. On the set, everyone had resumed their positions. The director was behind the camera and Chloë Rose was on her horse looking off into the distance. There was stillness as everyone waited, trying not to shuffle their feet or cough. Chloë's lips moved, a beat went by, and then everyone else moved again.

"It's still amazing to me how small these sets are when they look so big in the cinema," Knox said.

Mandy Ehrhardt was coming our way with the boy trailing behind her. She was moving as though a bee had stung her.

"Maybe they're done after all," Knox said, and leaned out of the cart, "Mandy, hey, Mandy, are they finishing?"

"No," Mandy said without stopping. "But I'm supposed to get the kid a candy bar in the commissary, because co-star apparently means gofer."

"You could get one for me too," Knox called after her.

She held up her hand with only one finger raised. The boy skipped a few steps to keep up with her.

"Too bad she didn't wait," Knox said, letting out the clutch on the cart. "We could have given her a ride."

The cart's engine made a buzzing sound as Knox made a U-turn. We were suddenly in Springfield or Livingston or any of a thousand other towns in the U.S. The street sign even said Main Street. That lasted about fifty yards before we were coursing down a Chicago city street, and after that a dirt road outside a medieval castle.

"So, what's really going on here, Knox? How about coming clean?"

The folds in his face deepened to show insult. "Why wouldn't I be honest with you?"

"I don't know. Why would the studio need to hire a private dick when it has its own security force?"

"Force? That's a laugh. It's me, two retirees, and a couple of kids that don't shave yet. And we're here for the lot, not to be round-the-clock protection for one actress."

"Is it protection I'm supposed to be offering or comfort? I forget which."

"Ah, nuts to you. Just cash the checks and be glad."

"That's fine if you're right and Rose has gotten spooked for no reason. But if she *is* being followed and something happens to her on my watch…"

Knox waved his right hand at me in dismissal. Nothing was going to happen. Didn't I know that?

I wondered why I was being so hard on him. There was no shame in working for the studios. It's not like my other clients never lied to me.

But there was something about an old friend handing out the lies that I just didn't like.

We were nearing the front of the studio lot, driving along with regular traffic now, limousines, delivery trucks, bicycles. The traffic noise out on the Boulevard wasn't kept off the lot by the gatehouse or the high wall.

After a time, Knox said, staring straight ahead, "Just go to the Rosenkrantz house this evening. I'll show you where on the map. She knows to expect you."

I nodded, and we rode along for a while more.

"That Mandy was really angry, wasn't she?" Knox said, shooting me a tentative grin. He wanted to show we were friends again, no hard feelings. "And that lover's spat with Rosenkrantz? His wife right there, too."

"You know these creative types. They're creative in everything they do."

"Of course Sturgeon seemed a little liberal with where his hands were too. Positioning her on the horse."

We pulled up to the security office, and I got out of the cart. "Now you're just being a gossip," I said.

The cart bounced on its shocks as Knox got out. He reached into his pocket and pulled out five twenty-dollar bills. My retainer.

I took the money. "Who's the male lead in the picture?" I said. "I didn't see an actor on the set."

"John Stark. They didn't need him today. He's probably out on his boat. Why?"

"Thought it might be worth getting his perspective on what's going on."

Knox's brow turned stormy again. "You're not asking anyone any questions. This isn't an investigation, it's a show. You understand what I'm saying to you? Look pretty for the camera."

"Okey."

That didn't seem to ease his concern. "I can trust you on this, Foster, right?"

I nodded and smiled and handed his lie right back to him. "Yeah," I said. "You can trust me."

FOUR

I had a few free hours on my hands, so I retrieved my car, and drove west on Sommerset. I left the windows open and the wind buffeted me, causing my shirt to flutter and my tie to dance. When the houses started to have enough acreage to farm on, I turned south on Montgomery, following it down the hill to the area San Angelinos called Soso, what the real estate men called Harper's Promise. Despite the ambivalent name this was a fine neighborhood with good-sized Victorian-style houses that a previous generation of movie stars had bought as starter homes before moving up in size and elevation. The only surprising thing was that Chloë Rose and her writer husband hadn't moved up themselves in the years since she'd displaced champagne as America's favorite French import.

I turned onto Highlawn Drive. They lived at the corner of Montgomery and Highlawn in a medium-sized house. The Montgomery side of the property was lined with a protective hedge two stories high, meant to afford some privacy, but the front lawn was open to view from the street. I drove past the house to the end of the block, made a K-turn, and parked on the street three houses down. Then I walked back along the sidewalk with my hands in my pockets.

Their Victorian was gaudy and ornate, and did not belong on the West Coast. The main color was purple, offset by white trim and trellises at every edge that could be decorated. The wide white pillars at the main entrance looked thick enough to give Samson a challenge. They supported a flat second-story porch with a screened entrance. There were wicker lawn furnishings on the porch with rain-stained canvas cushions that looked unused. Anyone who wanted to get some sun at this house would use the backyard, out of view.

The flowerbeds were as gaudy as the house, a choice the landscape designer probably thought was complimentary. There were crocuses and lilies and daffodils and a few others that I couldn't name. They were arranged in a concentric kidney bean pattern to either side of the walk. There was a detached garage that appeared to be a late addition. While it was also painted purple and white, its design was too utilitarian for the Victorians, practically a shed. The doors were open to reveal a maroon LaSalle coupe and an empty spot for a second car.

The backyard was much the same as the front, only the flowerbeds here were butterfly wings. An automatic sprinkler ratcheted around in a ticking pattern, keeping time with long arcs of water. Since I'd left my raincoat home, I decided to skip the backyard for now and check the garage first. It was built on a slab of poured concrete that looked practically scrubbed clean. There wasn't even a spot of oil where the missing car should have been. The walls were covered in pegboards with hooks to hold every tool a servant might need around the property. A wooden bench against the back wall was lined with mason jars holding screws, nails, bolts, hinges, and other hardware. I went to the coupe and opened the door. The registration was in the name of "Clotilde-ma-Fleur Rosenkrantz." I could see why she had chosen a stage name.

"That's about enough," a man said behind me.

I pulled out of the car, but didn't close the door. A short, squat Mexican stood backlit in the entrance of the garage. He wore a red velvet dinner jacket that was too big for him and matching pants that were cuffed at the bottom. His hair was combed straight back from his forehead and plastered in place. He was a young man, old enough to show a little class but not so old that he couldn't best you in a fight. Just your average Mexican. The Luger in his right hand didn't hurt his chances either.

I brought my hands around to where he could see them. "You know, if you point those things at people, somebody's liable to get hurt."

"Who are you?" He had almost no accent.

"My name's Dennis Foster. It's all right. I'm working for Miss Rose."

"Nobody works for the Rosenkrantzes but me, and I don't know you."

"I just got hired today, at the studio," I said.

His gun held steady. "Try another one."

"I don't have another one. That one's the truth. You mind pointing that gun somewhere other than at me? This suit doesn't need any more holes in it."

"Move away from the car. Close the door. And then get off the property before I call the police."

"I get it. You've got the gun, I have to do what you tell me. But if you were really to shoot me, whose side do you think the police would be on?"

His dark face grew darker.

"Look, we work for the same people. No need to act tough."

"I've got my instructions," he said. "Miss Rose was very clear: I am to watch for people that don't belong here. Now I find you in her car. What does that sound like to you?"

"It sounds like the same thing the studio hired me for. To look for people that don't belong around here. I'm a private detective."

He was still unconvinced. "Nobody said anything to me about a dick."

"Well, maybe you're not privy to every last thing that goes on. Hell, maybe I should ask who you are. How do I know you work for the Rosenkrantzes?"

He didn't like that. "Get going. Scram." When I didn't, his voice rose. "I said get out of here."

"Sure. If they have you, what would they need to hire a dick for? You're tough no matter which side of the bed you got up on."

"Enough talking." He moved the gun to call attention to it in case I had forgotten it was there.

"Look, I'll show you my license. I'm going for my wallet here." He held the gun out further as I reached for my pocket. I got out the Photostat of my license and held it towards him.

He took a few steps forward, turning his body so that the gun stayed out of my reach as he took my license. He resumed his position and then looked at it. "This doesn't prove anything. You could have gotten that anywhere, and even if it's yours, it doesn't tell me who you're working for."

I held my hands up in defeat. "You're right. I didn't know they made Mexicans as smart as you. I thought you were just good for a little music and handing out drinks."

"You think that's funny?" His accent showed more when he got angry.

"Not especially," I said. "Listen, if you'll aim that pea-shooter somewhere else and give the license back, I'll be on my way. We can sort this out later when your boss is at home."

He twitched the gun in the direction of the open garage door but didn't lower it.

"My license?"

He tossed it at my chest. I caught it on the rebound and pocketed it.

"Out," he said.

I edged along with my back to the LaSalle and my hands held high. I'd left the car door open. He followed me with his gun. He was intent on his job.

When I stepped out into the sun, the Mexican seemed to disappear in the shadows of the garage. I assumed the gun was still trained on me. I wondered what his duties actually were. He wasn't driving the car that was gone and he wasn't dressed for yard work. He made a good watchdog, though. It kind of made me wonder why they needed me.

The sprinkler had finished its artificial rainfall, and now it was just a quiet neighborhood without a sound except for the occasional car going by or airplane overhead or delivery being made. It was a nice part of town to live in, safe but not too presumptuous. I strolled along the drive, taking my time about it, just to give the Mexican something else to be angry about. I heard the LaSalle's door slam and then the sound of the garage doors closing. Out on the street, there wasn't a single person in evidence. The whole neighborhood looked like a set. I walked along to my car, got in, and started the motor.

FIVE

North of Sommerset were the Hills. The more money you had, the higher up you got to dig your foundation. Here there were landscaping teams in canvas slacks and bandanas at work on every third yard, and that was just counting the yards that could be seen from the street. There were probably gardeners working on half of the homes that were hedged or walled or gated too. These were the winter palaces of Hollywood's royalty, large Spanish-style mansions dating back to the silent era, southern plantation-style homes from the rise of the talkies, angular mesa homes clinging to precipices for the newly rich. There might have been competition between the residents, but to an outsider, the whole enclave represented those who had the money. To the moneyed, it was probably a much too thin line of defense against the masses.

Several blocks into the development, I stopped along the side of the road, idling in the shadow of a hedge. I only had to wait a few minutes before an open-topped tourist bus drove by, the amplified voice of the tour leader pointing out the homes of the stars. I pulled in close enough so I could hear the tour guide's patter, a cheerful droning of names sprinkled with months-old gossip that had been de-clawed for the out-of-towners. The bus wove its way along the narrow curving street, intent on covering every inch of pavement that had been blessed with the magic of the movies. When the tour guide eventually said John Stark's name, I tapped the brake and let the bus pull on ahead of me. I was glad to be rid of it. I had swallowed enough exhaust for one day.

Stark's home was open to view. There was a lush expanse of emerald grass venturing up a hill to the house. A circular drive was hidden from the street, which gave the impression that the grass went right up to the mansion's front door. The architect had placed two white columns on either side of the door, and had probably thought it added a touch of antiquity, but mostly it made him look like he was angling to see his work memorialized the next time they re-did the back of the five-dollar bill. The house behind the columns was little more than a sprawling box. It was painted white with decorative black shutters pinioned to the left and right of every window. It was the kind of home that would have a candle lit in each window at Christmastime and a big imported wreath on the front door. It was a modest abode. No more than thirty rooms at the outside.

I pulled up the steep drive until I was even with the front door. There was a short step up to a platform made from a single slate slab. I rang the bell and heard the distant sound of chimes within. The light hanging from the top of the portico looked as heavy as a car, and I made sure to be out from under it as I waited for someone to answer the door.

I was just reaching for the bell again when the door opened. A pretty young man with fair hair and a perfectly even bronze tan stood in the entry. His jaw and his eyes showed that he was fully grown, but there was something about him that remained boyish. Maybe it was the unmarked skin and the hint of down on his cheeks or maybe it was his slender body. He was dressed in pale blue suit pants but with no jacket or tie. It was hard to tell if he was a member of the house staff or a guest. His expression was of minor annoyance. "Yes?"

"Dennis Foster." I held out one of my cards. He didn't reach for it. "I was hired by the studio over a matter of security. I wanted to ask Mr. Stark some questions."

His expression changed to boredom, and he closed the door without a word.

I stood still for a moment, the door too close to my face. I considered ringing the bell again. The man hadn't said that Stark wasn't at home. Then I turned to look down the hill to the street. Everything was green. No one was in sight.

I was considering my options when the door opened behind me. It was the same young man, his expression of boredom now extending over his whole body. I decided he must not be a member of the staff with such an unprofessional disposition. He moved to a position alongside of the door and waved his hand towards himself. "Come on. Come in."

I stepped inside and he closed the door behind me. The entry hall's ceiling went to the roof. The floor was gray marble, and it kept the room cool. It was just large enough to walk your dog without having to go outside. There were two large archways on either side of the hall, and a massive marble staircase directly across from the front door that went up to a landing and then divided, continuing up to the right and the left. He walked around me and started diagonally towards one of the farther archways. His footsteps gave a dull echo.

"You don't go in for much security here," I said.

"People know better than to come."

"Much trouble with the staff?"

He ignored that question. He led me through a sitting room decorated in white and yellow, through a music room with floor-to-ceiling wood slat shades along two walls, and then through a small doorway onto a verandah that looked out on what would have made a good eighteenth hole.

"Presenting this guy, Johnny," the pretty man said with a dismissive flick of his wrist. He went to the edge of the verandah and leaned against one of the white pillars, facing me, with his arms crossed. Definitely not a member of the staff.

Johnny Stark, the face loved by millions, sat in Bermuda shorts and a lemon-colored golf shirt on a large white wicker chair, his bare feet on a matching wicker ottoman. Leather sandals lay neatly on the floor beside him. His dark hair, his cleft chin, his white teeth were all perfect, just like in the pictures. He didn't even seem smaller. He had an open manuscript on his lap, the already-read pages bent back behind the pages remaining to be read. A glass on a table beside him could have been iced tea with a twist of lemon or iced tea with a fifth of vodka. I wasn't close enough to tell. He looked at me with a wide smile and raised eyebrows.

"Your man tell you why I'm here?" I said.

That got a rise out of the fellow holding up the pillar.

His hands went to his hips and his mouth opened wide. "Now what is that supposed to mean?"

"Greg," Stark said, making a calming gesture with his hand, and then I knew how it was.

"So are you on the payroll?" I said with a smile.

Greg's hands went up in exasperation. "Johnny—"

"Shhhh," Stark said. Greg crossed his arms again and made a show out of his sulk. Stark turned that gorgeous smile on me. How many women had it made fawn over him? How many men? "Mr. Foster, Greg *is* on the payroll. He works in the kitchen. But the staff is off this afternoon. Can I get you a drink? We don't usually get unexpected visitors—"

"Even with no gates on the drive?"

"Mr. Foster, the gates are invisible and they're much further away than just my drive."

"I'll make do without the drink, thank you."

He shrugged with indifference.

"The studio hired me to look after Chloë Rose, Mr. Stark. Apparently she's being followed and she's worried for her safety. I'm trying to find out if anyone else has seen this man she says is following her. You notice anyone hanging around the set that doesn't belong?"

"Well it takes a lot of people to make a movie…"

"It could even be someone who works for the studio, but doesn't work on your picture, or someone on your picture that would make Miss Rose nervous for some reason."

He smiled at that and shot his eyes across at Greg who had let his indignation go, but still held his arms across his chest.

"Did I say something funny?"

"Have you met Chloë yet?"

"Al Knox tried to introduce us this afternoon. It didn't work out."

He laughed then, an open laugh that showed all of his teeth. "I'm sorry, Mr. Foster, it's just that it doesn't take a lot to make Chloë Rose nervous."

"Does she have reason to be?"

"Do any of us have reason to be? Certainly. We all do. You do too. Everyone. But that doesn't mean I am nervous. Are you?"

"I'd appreciate an answer to my question still."

Greg tsked and uncrossed and recrossed his arms.

Stark's eyes went up, and he said, "No, I haven't noticed anyone around the set that I would say didn't belong there. I know that Chloë thinks there is someone, but she's never pointed him out to me."

"So you think she's making it up?"

"She might be mistaken," he said diplomatically. He took a deep breath and then said, "I have been threatened and I have been followed. The price of fame. But it doesn't happen nearly as often as you'd think it might and it's never as sinister as you fear. Chloë's just skittish."

"You mean crazy."

"Actresses are their own animal," he said. "May I ask why the studio has hired a private detective to protect Chloë instead of making use of someone already on staff?"

"You'll have to ask someone at the studio that, and if you get an answer, feel free to tell me."

"See, Greg," Stark said, shooting out his hand toward the other man, "we're all good friends."

Greg tried to bolster his gloomy disposition, but it didn't look genuine.

"Was there anything else, Mr. Foster? You just wanted to know if I had seen any shady characters? I feel like we're in a movie."

"That's it," I said. "No one's given me any more to go on."

"Why don't you go ahead and meet Chloë, and then do what everyone in S.A. with brains does, take the studio's money."

"Thanks for the advice." I leaned forward and floated my card onto the table beside his drink. "I'm sure we'll be seeing each other again. I can show myself out." I didn't wait for either of them to move, just headed back into the house. Behind me, I could hear Greg's higher-pitched voice begin to whine. Part of me wanted to frisk the house just on principle, but in a place that size no more than two or three of the rooms are personal, and it would take too long to find them. I went out to the car, and rolled down the drive without having to touch the gas.

SIX

At seven o'clock I was back at the Rosenkrantz place. The house at night looked much like the house during the day, only with enough lamps blazing to light the Queen Elizabeth. There were lights upstairs and lights downstairs. There were mushroom-shaped guide lights along the front walk and two high-powered spots for the front lawn. There was another spotlight shining from the roof onto the drive. If you intended to sneak up on the Rosenkrantzes, you didn't want to do it dressed in burglar black.

I took the front stairs this time. I had on my good suit, a navy blue so deep it looked black, with a pressed white shirt, a red-and-blue-striped tie, a red handkerchief, and freshly polished loafers. I'd had a shower and a shave. It was five minutes after seven. The front door opened before I rang. It was my friend from the afternoon, without the gun this time.

"They let you in here too?" I said. "I didn't know it was that kind of place."

He stepped back to let me pass. "Mr. Foster."

I went in and took off my hat. "I guess they only allow artillery at the servant's entrance. It's certainly more welcoming this way."

He closed the door. "This time Miss Rose let me know

you were expected." He hesitated a moment. "I'm sorry about…"

"That's okay," I said. "I like to have people point guns at me every once in a while. Reminds me I'm still alive."

He gave a slight nod, and vanished through the archway on the left without a word.

The front hall was open to the second-floor ceiling, where a tarnished bronze chandelier cast just enough light to make the space gloomy. The front door was set between twin staircases that led up to a catwalk hallway. There were three doors on the catwalk along with the French doors directly overhead that opened to the up-stairs patio. The floor was largely covered with overlapping Persian rugs that bore the marks of foot traffic from each of the stairwells to the squared arches off to the left and right. Here and there rich maroon tiles could be seen where the floor was exposed. Two large breakfronts at the back of the hall were stuffed with books and porcelain dolls.

The sound of men laughing burst forth from one of the upstairs rooms. It was a frantic sound that suggested alcohol.

The Mexican came back. "Miss Rose, she's not feeling very well tonight."

"I'm sorry to hear that."

"She won't see you tonight." He smiled. "Maybe to-morrow."

"Of course," I said. "We all serve at her pleasure." I started to fit my hat back on my head when a telephone rang with extensions in several of the rooms. The Mexican and I stared at each other in the silence only a ringing telephone can create. Then he said, "Excuse me," and went back through the archway from which he had come.

The noise stopped, and then Shem Rosenkrantz stumbled out of one of the upstairs rooms calling "Clotilde...." He was in his shirtsleeves with black suspenders holding up pants that sagged in the middle. His face was red from drinking too much and his nose was covered with broken blood vessels from drinking too often. His straw hair was parted down the center. He looked like a stereotype of the great American author, which is what he was. "Clotilde... It's that man again about your damn horse!" He saw me then and stopped. "Who the hell are you?"

I tipped my hat. "Just one of the hired help."

"Well tell my wife to answer the damn phone," and he headed back into the room.

I thought about that for a moment and decided Rosenkrantz's order overrode the Mexican's plea of Chloë Rose's frailty. I followed where the servant had gone and was in the dining room when I heard him say in some further-off room, "The telephone, miss." I stopped, and her voice said something I couldn't make out. I looked around the room. There was a phone extension on the sideboard. I went to the phone and picked it up, covering the mouthpiece with my hand.

"I've told you before," Chloë Rose said, "Constant Comfort is not for sale."

I grabbed a pencil by the phone and scrawled "Constant Comfort" on the top sheet of the notepad lying beneath it.

"He'll give you *three* horses in trade, good horses, and he said that you can renegotiate your contract."

"I don't care what he said, he should have the decency to call me himself. And the answer is no, you little," she hesitated to think and then spat, "pissant."

"Hold on, Miss Rose, we're all working for the same guy."

"That's right, working for him, not owned by him. Good evening."

The phone rang off, although I could still hear the man breathing. He could probably hear me. I gently replaced the receiver on the base, tore the top sheet off the pad and pocketed it, and then walked casually out of the room into the front hall. A minute later, the Mexican emerged as well from where he had no doubt had to hold the phone for the ailing Chloë Rose so the weight wouldn't strain her. "Nice place," I said, looking up with my hands in my pockets as though I were admiring the moldings. "Some real nice pieces in there," indicating the other archway with my head, cool and convincing as a long-nosed dummy. "Well, I'll be in my car down the street if I'm needed," and I took the main entrance before he could respond.

I walked the mushroom-lighted path to the street, and then down the middle of the street to my car. It was almost as hot outside as it had been at noon. A perfect night for car sitting, if you were cold-blooded. I got in behind the steering wheel and rolled down the windows on both sides. I thought about breaking the first rule of a nighttime stakeout and lighting a cigarette and decided that it didn't matter if I got spotted. The whole job was cockeyed already. A stakeout and follow job required two people for it to be done properly. And I hadn't even been granted access to my client, Knox's assurances notwithstanding. The only way those two facts added up to something that made sense was if I really was just here for show, a piece of set decoration, and not a very necessary one either. This case already had a mystery man on the set, a mystery man on the phone, the mystery man that the man on the phone was bargaining for, the mystery man who was drinking and laughing with Shem Rosenkrantz upstairs. I was one too many. I felt like I had come to the party late and got seated at the wrong table.

I took out a match and lit it on my thumbnail the first time. I took a drag of my cigarette and watched the tip glow orange. I thought about the phone call. I didn't know what to make of it or even if there was anything to make of it. It was your regular strong-arm phone call. All of the up-to-date movie stars got them. They found it invigorating.

I smoked and watched as one by one the inside lights went out in each of the houses on the block. The outdoor lighting gave the neighborhood an ominous look. At nine, the Mexican came out and walked towards Montgomery. He would catch the Number 3 bus on Sommerset to go home. At 11:30, a police cruiser came around, right on time. It pulled up alongside me and I had to get out my license and laugh at a few corny jokes before they went away. I must have lit at least three more cigarettes, but I wasn't counting. My mouth felt like cotton. I wouldn't have turned down a drink.

Eventually the lights downstairs went out. The front hallway chandelier went next. I waited for the upstairs rooms. If there had been two people laughing when I first came in, and I thought there had been, then someone should be ready to come out just about now, or they had a houseguest that I should have known about. That was if there had been two voices. It could have been the radio.

A car started at the back of the house. I could make out the taillights through the next-door neighbors' hedge as it backed out down the drive. It wasn't the LaSalle I had seen earlier; this was a tan Buick sedan. It pulled out into the street facing me, which gave me a clear view of the driver: Shem Rosenkrantz, his face bloated and sour with drink. Someone was sitting in the passenger seat next to him and when the car passed under a streetlight, I caught the passenger full in the face: Hub Gilplaine. That was Hub Gilplaine the nightclub owner, casino operator, and publisher of pornographic books—the sort with more words than pictures, if that made any difference. I knew him by sight on account of how often he got his picture in the paper for donating to one charity or another. He sat tense and upright, his face pinched, clearly worried for his safety with Rosenkrantz at the wheel, and with good reason.

The glare of the Buick's headlights brightened my windows as the sound of their motor went by and then darkness and the engine draining away. I looked behind me in time to see them turn left at the next block. It would take them out of the development to one of the major arteries, Woodsheer or Sommerset. I looked at the house, and saw each of the upstairs windows go dark.

Chloë Rose was in for the night. But Shem Rosenkrantz was out with a known pornographer. And he was in no condition to drive. Some concerned citizen had to make sure they were safe. I started my car and swung around in a wide U-turn.

SEVEN

I caught up with them just as they turned east on Woodsheer. The boulevard was busy enough, even at that hour, for me to keep a car between us at all times. They took Woodsheer out of the quiet prestige of the Hills and into the glut of traffic that was the Mile. As the traffic lights coyly winked, Rosenkrantz drove in fits and jerks, enough to make the most stoic traffic cop swallow his whistle. The retail stores were closed, but people weren't out in the middle of the night to do any shopping. At least not the sort of shopping done in a store. Women in sheer satin blouses and once sensible skirts now covered with spangles strolled alongside men with loud patterned suits and wide-brimmed hats on their way from the fights or to the club or just on their way. These pedestrians had no regard for the traffic, which provided Rosenkrantz several opportunities to turn my knuckles white on the steering wheel.

We managed to reach the comparative safety of Los Bolcanes without incident, and from there we drove all the way out to Aceveda–Route 6. Route 6 took us north, out of San Angelo, into the San Gabriel Mountains. I knew then we were on our way to Arcucia, but I let them lead the way. Hub Gilplaine had a club in Hollywood for all of the movie people to be seen in called The Tip. There were waiters in tuxedoes and a fountain in the middle of the dance floor, and five-course meals, and a mixed jazz band to add a little spice. It made a nice background for when you had your picture taken. But if you wanted a real good time you went to his other operation, the Carrot-Top Club, a casino out in Arcucia, not far from the Santa Theresa racetrack. Players could lose some money at one and then go lose some more at the other.

Rosenkrantz drove on and so did I. It was cooler in the mountains. The road was cut through or dangled over the peaks and rises of the landscape. As the suburbs petered out, larger houses appeared, perched on large parcels of land to either side of the road. We passed a field of cows huddling together in a tight group that shifted in trips of unsteady hooves. There was an orchard that must have been apple trees since this wasn't good land for oranges, and then some more animals roaming free behind a wooden fence. It was impossible to hide in country like that. I tried to leave half a mile between us, but that was just for show, I knew they knew I was there. But it was a public road. I had a right to ride on it. I was just another customer.

After several empty miles, the road curved around an outgrowth of rock and suddenly a smattering of lights could be seen in the valley below. These were the homes of the respectable citizens of Arcucia who had lobbied against the legalization of horse racing but who rolled over for Gilplaine once the track was built. Once you've let a little sin into your life, what's the problem with a little more? The signs warned us to slow down and a moment later, evenly spaced bungalows with pebbled drives and postage stamp lawns lined the road. We sped through the ghost town that was the downtown district, then on to more residential spreads. These homes were a bit larger and set back from the road with woodland around them. There was an uninterrupted spate of trees, and then the Buick turned onto an unmarked back road whose entrance was no more than a gap in the forest, a black cavern out of Grimm.

I followed. There was nothing but dark all around. The headlights of my car lit the road just far enough for me to see something before I hit it. I kept my eyes on the other car's red taillights. Pockets of fog sat in the road's depressions giving the feeling that the woods were closing in. There was a flash, and then a car coming the other direction squeaked by without slowing down. There might have been lights in the distance behind me. Why not? The Carrot-Top did good business.

The Buick slowed and turned off at an angle onto another uneven dirt road. The impression of seclusion was damaged somewhat by the lights from the town now just visible through the woods. As remote as it felt, we were still in civilization. Of course, it had the trappings of exclusivity necessary to make the paying customers feel special. There was probably a secret password at the door. And men in funny hats. And every other word spoken would mean something other than what the word really meant—words like 'tea' and 'horse.' The cops would want it that way too. I had a feeling they weren't going to like me.

A clearing opened up where gravel had been put down and about thirty cars were parked in neat lines. I pulled into the first empty spot I saw, while the Buick drove up

to the front door and Rosenkrantz and Gilplaine turned
the car over to the valet. I waited for them to disappear
through the front door before I got out of my car.

The Carrot-Top Club had originally been built as the
guest house of a mountain retreat for some new-money
oil millionaire who lost the property when his money ran
out. Gilplaine had gotten it cheap at auction. It was a
two-story frontier home with unpainted cedar shingles and
a slate roof. A canopied porch of wooden planks ran the
entire length of the front of the house with two rocking
chairs still off to the side waiting for ma and pa. There
were two windows to either side of the door and three
more upstairs, all blocked by blackout curtains, which
left the parking lot shrouded in night, except where the
open front door cast a yellow carpet of light leading into
the club.

I arrived at the door just as the valet returned from
parking the Buick. A dark-haired sharp in a tuxedo
stopped me in the doorway and tapped my shoulder clip.
"No guns."

"This? I just wear it out of habit. It's like my wallet."

The tuxedo gave me a smile and held out his hand. "I'll
take good care of it for you."

"Like hell you will," I said and walked away from the
door. I peeled off my coat, unbuckled my shoulder holster,
and tucked the whole thing under the passenger seat of
my car. When I got back to the front door, neither the
tuxedo nor the valet so much as looked at me as I entered.

Inside, the whole first floor was one large open room
about the size of a small ballroom, with exposed support
beams and a stairway in the middle going up to the second

floor. A mahogany bar lined one wall, its mirror doubling the four rows of liquor bottles. That part was all strictly legal now, although the bar was scuffed enough to suggest that it had been dependable through Prohibition too. The bar's brass edges could have used a shine. That didn't prevent half of the barstools from being filled with dark-suited men and women in cocktail dresses shouting over one another to be heard.

The other side of the room was where the real action was. There were three blackjack stations, two craps tables, and a roulette wheel. The dealers wore red vests with brass buttons and black bowties. Small crowds of boisterous onlookers partially hid the gaming tables. The sound of the ball skittering around the roulette wheel could be heard over the noise of excited conversaton. There was no band. No one would have listened to them if there had been one, so Gilplaine probably figured he might just as well save the cost.

I went to the bar first. As I did, a heavyweight champion in an ill-fitting suit followed after me. I leaned against the bar and he leaned against it right next to me. It was an empty space. No reason he shouldn't lean against it.

I caught the bartender's eye and ordered a Scotch. I scanned the room while he poured my drink. There was no sign of Rosenkrantz or Gilplaine. I tasted my Scotch. It was too good for me, but the studio was picking up my expenses. I paid and started for the nearest blackjack table. My oversized shadow followed with all of the subtlety of a white suit at a funeral. I watched several hands and for all I know so did he. The house went over once, hit blackjack twice, and paid out to a dealt blackjack once. I thought I'd check on the other tables just to make sure that my new friend got his exercise. At the craps table, he stood so close I could feel his breath on the back of my neck. I turned and looked at him, but he just smiled a closed-mouth smile. I showed him all of my teeth, then turned back to the game.

When I had had enough of that, I went around to the other side of the table, crossed behind the croupier at the roulette wheel, squeezed past a couple leaning against the wall, and hurried over to the stairs. I was only halfway up when the heavyweight's tread sounded behind me. I turned and was able to look him in the eye from two steps up. "Did somebody stick a candy on my back?"

He grinned again. "I'd've thought your mother'd have taught you the golden rule."

"I know a few golden rules. Which one do you mean?"

"Treat others the way you'd want 'em to treat you back."

"Yeah, I've heard that one," I said. "I don't remember following you though."

This time he showed me that he was missing a few of his teeth.

"Yeah, well," I said, "then it's time to switch places. You take the lead and I'll follow you to Gilplaine's office."

The heavyweight raised his chin. "You'll find it. It's the second door on the left. I'll be right behind you in case you get scared."

I thought of something smart to say to that, but then I remembered I wasn't smart, so I just turned up the stairs.

EIGHT

Gilplaine's office looked like a storage room with a desk stranded in the center. Three of the walls were lined with brown cardboard boxes that had been labeled in a scrawl with the titles of erotic pulp novels: *Leslie's Love*, *I Married a Man's Man*, *Never Enough*, that kind of thing. The musty smell of old cheap paper filled the room, somewhere between a library and a locker room. There was a couch along the fourth wall, itself half covered in boxes, and three tall green filing cabinets taking up valuable real estate. Rosenkrantz, still dressed as informally as he had been at the house, occupied the free spot on the couch.

Gilplaine sat at his desk, leaning back in a swivel chair, its spring audibly protesting his weight. He was a sharp-faced man, with a head twice as high as it was wide. This had the effect of making his nose seem longer than it was, which didn't inspire any confidence in his honesty. He had piercing dark eyes that he focused with all of his attention on only one thing at a time. He wore an army-green three-piece suit with a gold chain coming out of the watch pocket and running to the gold watch in his hand. He looked at it, making note of the time, before placing it open on the desk blotter in front of him where he could consult it with a minimum sacrifice of attention. "What do you want?" he said.

"Hold on, I know him," Rosenkrantz said. The drive must have sobered him, since his speech no longer showed any sign of alcohol.

"You do?" Gilplaine said without taking his eyes off of mine.

"He was at the house before."

"Yes, he followed us when we left."

"No, inside the house. He's the detective they hired for Clotilde."

"Well, Mister…?"

I handed over a card, and he glanced at it.

"Well, Mr. Foster, you don't seem to be doing a very good job of protecting Miss Rose."

"How do you figure that?" I said.

"Right now, for instance, you're here with us."

"Maybe you're the ones she needs protecting from."

His eyes darted to the watch and then back to me.

"Just throw him out, Hub," Rosenkrantz said.

Gilplaine moved his mouth like he had just tasted something sour. "My men tell me you tried to bring a gun into my club."

I shrugged. "I thought I might need it."

"And what do you think now?"

"I was right."

"Are you certain you want to make an enemy of me, Mr. Foster?"

"No. But I am certain there isn't much that's honest about you. I'm certain you're a dirty little man who makes his money in dirty things for dirty people. I'm certain that a man like you anywhere near Miss Rose is something to protect her from."

Gilplaine's eyes narrowed. The champ shifted behind me and the floor creaked.

"Hah," Rosenkrantz said. "I should be writing this stuff down." He patted his pockets for something to write on.

Gilplaine continued to consider me with the scrutiny a mother gives her child before the first day of school. Then his face loosened and he spoke quickly. "Mr. Rosenkrantz and I are business acquaintances. Mr. Rosenkrantz is a writer, I am a publisher. We are discussing a forthcoming book. None of it has anything to do with his wife. Is that satisfactory?"

I shrugged.

"Not that it's any of your business. But if we get this straight now, I hope you won't go on annoying me in the future." Gilplaine looked once more at his watch and then clicked it shut. "Listen, Mr. Foster. I don't like cops who think they're smart when they're not. I don't like cops who think they're clean when they're not. I don't like cops who talk out of turn, and I don't like cops who talk in turn."

"Since we're all being so honest here," I said, "you have any ideas about who's been following Miss Rose?"

Rosenkrantz had found a notepad and was jotting notes with a golf pencil.

"Why would I have any idea about that?" Gilplaine said. "I'm not involved with the movies, even if my business sometimes involves people who are. I don't know who'd be following her around."

"No one's following her, Hub. Clotilde is imagining it," Rosenkrantz said. And to me he said, "You're busting yourself up for nothing. Just sit in your car and watch her and collect your money."

"That's what people keep telling me," I said.

"I have no information about this," Gilplaine said. He picked up his watch and tucked it away in his pocket. "And you've taken up all the time I care to give you."

The chair squealed as he turned to face Rosenkrantz. "Where were we, Shem?"

The creaking floor warned me to step out of the way before Hub's man could get a grip on my shoulder. "I'll walk myself out," I told him. "That's one thing my mother did teach me."

He grinned that same closed-mouth grin that could have meant that he found me amusing or might just have meant that he had gotten hit in the head one too many times. He opened the door, and I stepped past him and hurried down the hall. I'd been wasting time, like the man said. Gilplaine was a publisher and Rosenkrantz a writer. It made sense that they would be working together, even though the critics would be surprised to find out that Rosenkrantz, the great golden boy, not only had sunk to writing for the pictures but even a step lower, writing for the under-the-counter trade.

Outside I went back to my car and sat behind the wheel without turning the ignition. I had been hired to sit in my car, as Rosenkrantz had reminded me, and Hub Gilplaine's parking lot was as good a place as any to sit. At the end of the night, Rosenkrantz and I were going back to the same place, after all. The Carrot-Top Club wasn't too particular about what time it closed, but it was late and it couldn't stay open forever. I lit a cigarette and listened to the crickets buzz in waves, the sound rising and receding. There was a light breeze, offering some relief from the heat in the valley. The smell of the trees was cloying. It made me miss the city.

Laughing groups and couples came out the front door and I watched the valet flitting around the lot. Headlights cut across the trees two by two as people made their way out. After an hour, about half of the cars were left. I could see the Buick several cars over. A breeze swept through the clearing and I shivered. I began to wonder if there was something back at the house that I shouldn't be missing. Just as I was about to start my engine, Rosenkrantz appeared in the doorway and handed the valet his ticket. He was alone. The valet ran off, and Rosenkrantz talked to the doorman while he waited. It was ten minutes to three.

I started my engine and backed out of the spot, pointing the nose of my car away from the club. I pulled onto the private back road just ahead of the Buick. Maybe if I was in front of him, he wouldn't notice he was being tailed. We retraced our route through the endless wall of trees, past the town, up into the mountains and Route 6, and then eventually into the city and Woodsheer. I thought it would be better for me not to go directly to the house, so I drove past Montgomery and turned in the next block. But as I did, I saw the Buick continue west on Woodsheer in my rearview mirror. I hurried around the block, but had to wait for passing traffic before I could follow.

I caught up with the Buick at a traffic signal. If Rosenkrantz was worried about being followed, he showed no sign, and took no measures to shake me. He pulled off the highway in Harbor City, a neighborhood of small one-family homes that had once been prosperous but was now mainly inhabited by people just off the bus who didn't know any better or people who couldn't afford to move out. All the windows were dark except for an occasional night owl up clipping coupons or crocheting a doily that couldn't wait for morning. He pulled into the driveway of the kind of bungalow that you could buy out of the Sears catalog. It had a small front porch, four small rooms on the first floor, and one small room upstairs. I knew that without going in. I'd been in houses like it. There was a Ford that had to be at least ten years old parked in front of him. No lights were on inside. I continued past, pulling along the curb almost at the end of the block.

I watched in my mirror as Rosenkrantz got out of the car, walked around the backside of it and went up the path to the door. He opened the screen and then let himself in with his own key. Maybe it was a bungalow he kept to do his writing in. Maybe he was an insomniac and could only write at three in the morning, with a pitcherful of liquor inside him. Maybe. I figured I'd give him a few minutes, and then I would go back over to Soso to finish the job I had been hired for. I could always come back and investigate the house during the day.

Less than a minute later Rosenkrantz burst out the front door and bolted to his car. The screen banged shut behind him. I heard the engine catch and then he backed out of the driveway fast enough to make the wheels scream. I waited a minute to see if anyone would take notice of the noise. The neighborhood was silent.

I got out of my car and walked to the house. On the way, I shined the small pen flash I kept in my pocket into the Ford, looking for the license holder, but I couldn't see it. I went up the walk, and pressed the doorbell. I could hear it buzz inside. Rosenkrantz had left the door wide open, and through the screen I had a dim view of the stairs to the second floor and a small entryway. No one answered the buzzer. I opened the screen door and went in.

I listened, but heard nothing. I swung the door closed and found a switch that turned on an overhead light. It lit the rooms to either side of the entrance enough for me to see old furniture in both, respectable but worn, and none of the pieces matching. I crossed into the living room and turned on one of the lamps on an end table. It was painted gold, but the gold had flecked in places revealing white ceramic beneath. There was a couch upholstered in tan, two chairs upholstered in different shades of blue. The floor was hardwood but a cord rug took up some of the space between the couch and the chairs. It had no doubt been advertised as a furnished house, and maybe it even commanded a few extra dollars for that.

I continued through the living room towards the back of the house where an open door let into a bedroom. The smell hit me before I turned on the light. I felt for a light switch beside the door, but didn't find any, so I got my pen flash again and waved it back and forth, painting the room with light. She was on the bed. The blood was from her neck and thighs. I forced myself to cross the room to the lamp on the bedside table. I turned it on, and recognized the face from that afternoon: Mandy Ehrhardt. A thin wool blanket had been pulled down to the foot of the bed and hung over onto the floor. She had bled out, and the sheets were sodden. This hadn't happened in the last five minutes. Which left Rosenkrantz in the clear. The rest of the room was a mess, clothing on the floor trailing out of the closet, a pile of shoes beside the bed, drawers left slightly open in the dresser, but it was the mess of a careless woman living in a room. There hadn't been any struggle. The room hadn't been searched.

I opened the drawer of the bedside table. It contained a comb and a brush, both with hair clinging to them, a small green jewelry box with a few inexpensive pieces of jewelry, a compact, and a makeup kit. I checked the dresser and the closet, but there was nothing but clothes. Miss Ehrhardt might have been in pictures, but she wasn't living the life of a star. I set everything as it had been before. When it looked right, I turned off the light. I went through the living room, past the front entrance into the dining room. The table was littered with movie magazines, some movie ticket stubs, used dishes, a glass with dark lipstick on the rim, bills, flyers. Her purse was there as well, but it contained nothing more interesting than her bedside table. Same with the kitchen.

I went upstairs. This room smelled dusty. There was a bed with a dropcloth over it. There was a stack of boxes, the lower ones caving in from the weight of the ones above. There was a roll-top desk and a swivel chair. There weren't any lights that worked. I went back downstairs, and turned off the lights there. Back in the vestibule, I thought about what reason I could give for being here. There wasn't any, except if you counted the truth. If I told it straight then I was Rosenkrantz's alibi, and maybe this could all stay away from his wife. On the other hand, if I called it in anonymously, my name would probably come into it anyway and then the cops would want to know why I had called it in anonymously in the first place. They didn't like an outside operator operating outside the role they gave to him. Knox wouldn't like it either. I cursed myself for being curious. I could have been sleeping in my car ten minutes away. I picked up the phone and dialed the police.

NINE

The cop who got it was a Harbor City homicide detective named Samuels. I didn't know him, but he took my story at face value and I liked him for it. He was a red-headed Irishman with piercing blue eyes and a spate of freckles from his hairline all the way down into his collar. His coat hung limp, like there wasn't much for it to hang on, but from watching him move it was clear that there was a lot of wiry strength there. He smoked cheap cigars that came in cellophane which he cut open with a pocket-knife, putting the cellophane back in his pocket. I liked him for that too. We stood in the dining room while the medical examiner and the photography boys took care of the body. He spoke quietly but forcefully.

"These Hollywood investigations are a farce. The studio will shut it down when they get wind of it tomorrow. Today, I guess."

"There are still a few hours before they have to hear of it," I said. "And it is murder. There's only so much that can be kept under wraps in a murder."

"Yeah, just who was murdered, and who did the murdering."

"The studio really has that much on you boys? I thought the law was untouchable in this town."

"Go on and laugh. Of course the studios can't order us to stop our investigation, but it seems that the bosses have a way of making it so that it should be a low priority with even a lower profile."

"The bosses," I said.

"The bosses." He smoked his cigar as the medical examiner, a young man with an expression of sobriety twice his age, went towards the front door with his bag. "You got anything for me, Doc?" Samuels said.

"She's dead," the ME said with his hand on the screen door's latch.

"That your professional opinion?"

The doc made a straight line of his mouth. "It was within the last six to eight hours. The cuts are all deep and inelegant."

"So this guy didn't know how to use a knife?" Samuels said.

"No, it looks more like he didn't know his own strength. The cuts are deliberate, no hesitation."

Samuels nodded and blew a plume of smoke.

"I'll have the rest once I get her on the table." And with that he went outside.

The sky might have been brighter out there or maybe I just hoped it was. "She have any family?" I said.

"An aunt and a grandma out in Wichita," Samuels said, flat.

"Isn't it always Wichita?"

"It always is." He paused. "You got any ideas you might be thinking of looking into on your own?"

"I was thinking of looking into a shower and then into

my bed, but maybe into a liquor store first if I can find
one that's open this early."

"Cut that and tell it to me straight, like you've been
doing up until now."

I sighed and shook my head. "I've barely been on this
thing longer than you have. This is just on the side of my
job."

"The job that is why you were following Rosenkrantz."

"Yeah."

"So it must have been a divorce job?"

I smiled but didn't say anything.

"You sure you can't tell me?"

"Not unless you can make me understand what it has
to do with this murder."

"How can I do that unless I know what the job was?"

"I guess you can't."

He squinted at me then and bit down on his cigar.
"The tech get your prints?"

"You've got them on file."

He nodded. "You can go then. Just don't leave town,
the usual story."

"I'll be right where you expect to find me."

"Yeah, well. Good night."

"Good morning, detective." We shook hands. I went
out the screen door into the chill of the morning. The sky
was starting to show purple at the edges, like a bruise. I'd
be able to see the sunrise if I could find a place to watch
it from.

My car had the bottled-up smell of sweat and stale
smoke. I rolled down the windows to let in the cool air

while it lasted, and started the engine. I had been hired to babysit a paranoid prima donna, and I had ended up finding a dead woman cut almost to pieces. For some reason, I felt as though I hadn't done a very good job.

I could at least try to make up for it. I pulled away from the curb and instead of heading back to Hollywood I took the turn at Montgomery.

TEN

The Rosenkrantz house looked undisturbed. I parked in the same spot I had the night before and killed the engine. The police would have to make a stop here later to get Rosenkrantz's testimony, but they weren't here yet. I got out of my car and walked up the middle of the road to the house. At the end of the drive, the garage doors were open and both the tan Buick and the maroon LaSalle were in their spots. I could check the house for signs of forced entry, but I didn't see the need. It was just a sleeping house in a sleeping neighborhood. There was nothing to see and no one had missed me. I went back to my car and leaned against the hood as I lit a cigarette. It took three tries to get the match going.

The Mexican arrived on foot just before seven wearing the same ill-fitting hand-me-down jacket of the day before. He saw me and came over.

"How was your night?" he said.

"Hot."

"Mine too."

We both let the silence take a turn. "My name's Miguel, by the way." He nodded toward the house. "I've got the dayshift now. You don't have to wait around."

"I'm just finishing my cigarette," I said, and took a drag.

He turned and crossed the street, on his way to his little castle where he got to protect the princess and there was trouble around every corner. I watched him go around to the back of the house. I waited another ten minutes to make sure he didn't come back out again with news of some tragedy, or at least a tragedy I didn't already know about. He didn't. The cops still hadn't shown up either. I finished my cigarette, got in my car, and pulled away.

In Hollywood, I stopped outside of the Olmstead without putting my car away in the garage. My apartment was just one big room with a private bathroom and a small kitchenette in a closet. I had done what I could to give each corner of the room its own purpose. There was a Formica table with two chrome chairs just outside the open kitchenette closet. There was a twin bed with a standing lamp and a night table just outside of the bathroom. There was my one good reading chair with another standing lamp and a stack of books on the floor over in the third corner. The only window was in the bathroom and it was made of pebbled glass.

I took three fingers of bourbon before my shower and another three after. I looked at the time and thought I ought to be hungry, so I went out again and stopped at a counter diner I liked and ordered a couple of scrambled eggs, hash browns, bacon, some well-burnt toast, and coffee, but the whole time I was working on it, I was thinking of a girl with her neck open and her thighs gouged out. I got down about half of my breakfast and left a good tip. I picked up the morning papers outside, but there was nothing in either of them about the Ehrhardt killing. It must have gotten called in too late.

The lobby of the Blackstone Building was empty. I took the automatic elevator up to the third floor. The hallway there was empty, too, and I was willing to bet that my office's unlocked waiting room would be empty as well. I was wrong. It had two too many people in it.

Benny Sturgeon stood as I came in, his hat held in both hands in front of his stomach like a shield. He was tall, but no taller than me. Up close there were flecks of white in his hair that made him look distinguished instead of aged. He wore a pair of glasses with circular frames that I had not seen on the set the day before. He was in shirtsleeves and a vest, and there were deep lines across his forehead and at the corners of his mouth.

Al Knox was already on his feet, pacing, a lit cigarette in one hand. His eyelids were heavy and his shoulders tilted forward as though his back couldn't support the weight of his stomach. He looked exactly like a man who had been woken early in the morning with bad news. I looked over at the standing ashtray covered in a fine layer of dust and saw that there was only one new butt. He hadn't been there too long.

"Now, Mr. Foster—" Sturgeon began.

"Dennis," Knox said.

"Mr. Foster, I must insist on seeing you first," Sturgeon started in again. He spoke with the conviction of a man used to giving orders that are obeyed. Only the way he held his hat ruined the effect. "I've come with a job of the utmost importance. It's imperative that we act right away."

I quieted him with a look I only took out on special occasions. "Al first, then you."

I stepped across to the inner door, unlocked it, and let Al into my office. I went around to my side of the desk and he sat down on one of the two straight-backed chairs on the other side. His lip curled.

"You're a bastard, you know that?"

I raised both my hands. "Al, I was following a legitimate lead…"

"They want Rose for it."

"What?" I felt as though someone had cut the cables on the elevator I was riding in.

"They want Chloë Rose for Mandy Ehrhardt's murder."

"Who do?"

"The cops. Who do you think?"

I leaned forward in my chair. "Al, I was at the scene. That was no woman's killing. Certainly not a woman of Chloë Rose's size. Can't the studio quash it?"

Al shook his head and ran a hand along his cheek, letting it slide off his chin. "She had the motive. Ehrhardt was sleeping with her husband. And thanks to you she doesn't have an alibi, but her husband does. The mayor doesn't like that the press says the SAPD turns a blind eye to the movie people. They don't like it in Harbor City much either. They're going to make an example of this one. There's no way they would convict a woman with Rose's looks, or one as famous as her—she's not even a citizen, for Christ's sake. So the press will feel they can ride it as hard as they want without anybody getting seriously hurt."

"Except for Mandy Ehrhardt, whose real killer walks away."

"And Chloë Rose's career, and the studio's bank account."

I sat back in my chair and lit a cigarette. "What do you mean she's not a citizen? She's married to Rosenkrantz, isn't she?"

"Resident alien. They met when he and his first wife were living in France. You ever hear how old she was?"

"How old?"

"The official story is eighteen. Unofficially, I've heard everything from seventeen to fifteen."

"So what? She's over eighteen now."

"So everything. It's all going to come out, how old she was or wasn't, and that story about what happened to her with some prison guard…"

"What prison guard?"

Knox waved a hand angrily. "I don't know, it's all rumors, but they're pretty nasty rumors. Mix that in with a murder trial here and see what you get. I'm telling you, there's plenty to feed the headlines for weeks. Months, maybe."

I shook my head, trying to reconcile the small, vulnerable, beautiful woman I'd seen the day before with the brutal mutilation and killing I had come across that morning. "It's all circumstantial."

"That's all they need. She's not supposed to hang for it. They make a big splash of her arrest, and if it never gets to a conviction, who cares? Only, we do care. We care plenty."

I just shook my head again.

"You really screwed up," Knox said.

"You came over just to tell me that in person?"

"That, and this: You're fired." He reached into the

inside pocket of his jacket, and pulled out an envelope. He tossed it on the desk. I left it there untouched.

He shook his head sadly. "I'm sorry, Dennis, I know we go way back, but—"

"You can skip the old friends bit. I heard it yesterday. I didn't like it then, and I like it even less now."

"Fine. Then just take the money and be glad you're not in deeper than you are." He mashed out his cigarette in my ashtray and stood up. He pointed at the door. "And if Sturgeon tries to get you to—"

"Oh, don't worry. I'm off the case."

At the door, Knox turned back with his hand on the knob. "We're not public servants anymore, Foster. We're not supposed to deal with this stuff anymore."

"We all serve someone," I said.

"I wish like hell I knew who you thought you were serving last night," he said. And he left the office, leaving the door open to the reception room, and slamming the outside door to the hall.

ELEVEN

I would have liked a moment to collect my thoughts before dealing with Sturgeon, but he was already in the open doorway. His hat was in one hand down at his side now. He had his chest out with his chin raised in a caricature of defiance. He was directing himself and he had lost the ability to realize he was hamming it up. When he started, his tone was stern. "Mr. Foster, I have a job for you."

I indicated the chairs across my desk. He sat on the one Knox hadn't.

"I assume Mr. Knox told you that they suspect Chloë of..." He took a deep breath. "Of what happened to Mandy."

I still had half a cigarette left, and I drew on it. "He did. What's that done to the picture?" I asked. "You're not filming today?"

He watched me smoke, but it was unclear if his expression was distaste or desire. I didn't offer him one. "With Mandy's death, and this business with the police and Chloë...I was forced to suspend filming for the morning. I'm shooting B-reel this afternoon."

"So the movie'll go on?"

"Mandy's parts were mostly finished. We'll just get

Shem to rewrite the few remaining scenes, and it should be fine."

"You mean Mr. Rosenkrantz, whose lover was killed last night, and whose wife is suspected of the killing. I'm sure he'll be eager to get to a typewriter."

His face showed his distaste. "Yes, I mean Shem Rosenkrantz. Now, what's with all the questions? I came to hire you. Don't you want me to let you know what the job is?"

I went on. "It must be a relief to you, that the picture will still get finished. You need this movie, don't you? Your career depends on it. Or was I misinformed?"

"What are you suggesting?"

"I'm not suggesting anything. Only that you have a pretty good reason not to want Chloë Rose to be on the hook for Miss Ehrhardt's murder. Especially if you were finished with Miss Ehrhardt anyway."

He stood. "I'm repulsed by your implication."

"What was my implication?" I said. "I must have missed it." Then I gave him the five-dollar smile.

Grudgingly he sat back down. "Don't you want to at least hear about the job?"

"You want me to prove that Chloë Rose did not kill Mandy Ehrhardt."

He tilted his head and gave a single downward nod. "That is correct."

"Well, I'm sorry, but I can't," I said.

"You can't? Mr. Foster, you're part of the reason she's in this mess, don't you want to get her out of it?"

"I just promised your chief of security that I was off this case. I don't want it anyway."

"Knox made you promise not to take my case?"

"Knox didn't make me do anything," I said, standing. "This whole thing was wrong from the start. All of you Hollywood people may be used to using each other like props, but I'm not a prop. I'm an honest guy trying to make a living. This story doesn't need me. My part was written out."

"You can't allow Chloë to have her career ruined, her life—"

"Skip it. Your picture'll get finished, and it'll even make a few extra dollars because it's got a dead ingénue in it. So don't start crying crocodile tears. My answer is no. Now if you don't mind."

He tried to push his chest out again, but it didn't work with me standing over him. He got up himself, to even things out. "I do mind," he said. "I'm willing to pay you quite a bit of money." He started fumbling at his pocket, at last coming up with a tan goatskin billfold. He took out a handful of bills.

I waved them away. "If you don't put that away, I might have to do something we'll both regret."

He stood there with the money in his outstretched hand just long enough to feel foolish. He put it away with one quick motion.

I picked up the envelope Knox had left on my desk and went over to the safe with it. "Had Miss Ehrhardt been in many other pictures?" I asked, just to be saying something.

"No, this would have been her first one, other than a few jobs as an extra."

I nodded as though that meant something to me, deposited the envelope in the safe, and locked it. Then I went over to the door and gestured for him to vacate my office. "You're welcome to use the reception room, but I've got work here."

He regarded me for a moment, deflated, and then stepped by me as though I were wet paint he had to worry about getting on his clothes. I pushed the door shut and locked it.

I listened, waiting for his exit. After a minute, I heard the outer door open and his footsteps grow faint in the hall. I could just make out the chime of the elevator when it arrived.

I looked around my office. I didn't have a damn thing to do. If I sat around long enough, maybe a client would come in, a fat heiress with a kidnapped dog, or a kid sister looking for her missing brother.

I hadn't decided about the check in the safe yet. It felt dirty to me. Studios didn't usually hire private investigators to follow their stars. The stars might themselves, but not the studio. And with the murder added in, the whole thing seemed like a setup to me. But who was getting set up? The obvious answer fell too close to home, but I couldn't figure it. There would have been no way to predict that I would have ended up in Harbor City last night at all. Something was wrong with this thing, and I wasn't going to figure out what standing around here.

I paced over to the safe and then back.

It's none of your business, Foster. You got paid off to let it drop.

Yeah, but the patsy costume doesn't quite fit right. It's too tight in the neck. And I'm not actually paid until I cash their check.

You're a damn fool, Foster.

That one I had no answer to. The only kinds of people in this business were fools who could admit it and fools who couldn't. I could admit it, but it didn't change what I was.

I started to unlock the door, but before the knob turned, the phone on my desk rang. I hesitated a moment, not eager to add whatever headache was on the phone to the ones I had been handed in the last five hours. But it rang again, insistent and impossible to ignore. I went back to my desk, and watched it ring a third time. I picked up from the client's side of the desk.

"Foster."

"Mr. Foster, we met yesterday." The voice was deep and charming and expertly controlled. "Do you know who I am?"

"I met a lot of people yesterday," I said. "So many that some aren't even alive today."

"This thing with Mandy is horrible," the voice said and I thought it sounded almost sincere. But who was I to judge? Maybe he was really shaken. Maybe he'd cried all morning.

"It's also keeping me busy. What do you want, Mr. Stark?"

"You do remember me! I suppose remembering people is important in your line of work." He paused to give me a chance to reply, but I didn't say anything. How many people forgot meeting John Stark? He went on, "I'm calling because Greg Taylor is missing. My...kitchen help. He answered the door for you yesterday."

"Yeah, I remember him too."

"I'm calling to see if you think you could find him. But you say you're busy..."

"How long has he been missing? He was there yesterday afternoon."

"Since shortly after you left. We had a fight, you see. He didn't like how you'd treated him and he thought I should have defended him better. Or that was the excuse for the fight. It had been almost two months since our last quarrel. It was bound to happen sooner rather than later. Anyway, he left, stayed away all night. He'll do that, but he always comes back in the morning. And with this thing with Mandy...I'm worried."

Now he sounded it.

"Why don't you go to the police? I'm sure for you they won't notice that it hasn't been twenty-four hours. They have a whole operation for this kind of thing."

"When Greg goes off like this, a lot of the things he does are not strictly legal. If he were in a compromising situation, I wouldn't want the police to be the ones who find him..."

Knox wanted me off the Rose/Ehrhardt case, and anything I had had in mind to do there was going to be strictly on my own time. Things weren't so good that I could turn away business.

Stark spoke into the silence, "I'd rather not go into more details over the phone."

"Of course you wouldn't," I said. "I take it you can't come to my office?"

"I was hoping you would come here."

"Right."

"They'll expect you at the door," he said, and he hung up.

Everyone wanted to keep me in this movie business. Everyone but the person who got me into it in the first place. I went through the routine with the lock and took the stairs so I wouldn't have to wait for the automatic elevator.

TWELVE

A proper butler opened the door at Stark's this time. He was bald with a horseshoe of hair around the back of his head, a pencil mustache, and a tuxedo with white gloves. He led the way across the marble entry hall, back through the same set of rooms I had seen the day before, and out onto the same verandah where Stark was in the same position. He was reading a different script, though, because only a few pages of this one had been turned back. Or maybe he was rereading his lines.

"He hasn't come back," he said, and tried his million-dollar smile, but his face looked pinched, and his eyes were afraid. He set the script down. "You will find him, won't you?"

"I charge twenty-five dollars a day plus expenses and I get one hundred dollars up front as a retainer."

His face lost any pretense now. He was very troubled. "That won't be a problem. That doesn't matter. He doesn't even need to come back. I just want to know that he's all right."

"You said he's done this before when you've fought. Where did he go?"

"He never gave me specifics. That was part of our un-spoken arrangement. He could go on an occasional bender but we would act as though it hadn't happened. I know that he would get high, shoot up."

"H?"

"Morphine, I think. Maybe it was heroin. His eyes were always glassy. Sometimes he'd end up with bruises on the insides of his arms. He's very delicate."

"Any friends, family he might have gone to?"

"I don't think so. Definitely no family. Greg isn't from San Angelo. Maybe friends, but I never met any. I know he would go to the Blacklight, Choices, all those Market clubs. If he was feeling lucky, maybe the Tip. He knew people who went there."

"Who?"

"Well, me, for one."

The Tip was Gilplaine's club. Of course it had to be the Tip. I didn't know the other places, but I wasn't the type who would know them. "Clubs close. He would have had to sleep somewhere."

"I told you. We never spoke about details."

"Do you have a photo of him?"

"No."

There was a sound at the door and I turned to find Vera Merton standing there in a bright red blouse with an oriental pattern and a muted red skirt that stopped just before the tops of her brown calfskin high-heeled boots.

"I step out for a moment, and I miss everything."

She touched my shoulder as she went past me and I caught the scent of cinnamon and cloves. She went around Stark's chair and settled herself in the one beside him, putting her boots up on the wicker ottoman.

"This is Mr. Foster," Stark said. "He's here about Greg."

She smiled, and her smile had no concern dampening it at all. "I think maybe we saw one another yesterday. Is that right?"

"Yes," I said.

She bit her lower lip and then said, "This has been a horrible horrible day." It sounded like the sort of thing she might say on a day when it rained too much.

Stark said, "I know that I'm not giving you very much information, but it's all I've got. I met Greg when he was nearly just off the bus and since then he's been living here. He didn't have much of a life outside of the house."

"And you never went out in public with him," I said.

He stiffened and said, "Not never. But rarely. I'm sure you'll understand, and you'll understand why this matter has to be kept private. If the studio hired you, I know you can be trusted."

"The studio doesn't feel that way this morning. I was the one who found Mandy Ehrhardt."

Miss Merton winced, almost as though she were remembering the ghastly scene herself.

Stark said, "I didn't know."

"Why would you have?" I said.

"Was it awful?" Miss Merton said, and now her face was pale and her voice unsteady.

"It always is," I said.

"Hey, Johnny," a man called from inside, and then appeared at the entrance to the porch. He was tall with dark hair, wearing dress pants and shirtsleeves, very neat, but the back of his shirt wasn't tucked in all of the way. He stopped short when he saw me, and ran his hand through his hair. I'd seen him yesterday, too.

"Tommy, this is Mr. Foster," Miss Merton said. "He's a private eye. Daddy hired him to look after Chloë."

"Oh?" Tommy said.

"But now I'm working for Mr. Stark," I said.

"John," Stark said, almost on reflex. "Please."

"Smashing," Tommy said. Up close, his breath carried a hint of gin on it as he exhaled. "I hope it all works out." He darted glances at each of us in turn. "Well, everybody…I need to see a man about a horse." And he gave a little bow with his head. As he walked, he faced backwards, pointing at Stark. "Don't you go anywhere, Johnny. We need to talk." Then he slipped inside the house.

"Is he always like that this early in the morning?" I said.

"What do you mean?" Miss Merton said.

"You know what I mean."

"Excuse me," Stark said. We both looked at him. "Can't we please get back to Greg? I'm concerned that he might have done something to hurt himself. With drugs or…" He shook his head and made a distasteful face. "I just want to make sure he's safe."

"And to get him to come back."

"If he wants to," Stark said. "But finding him is what matters. At least you've seen Greg, which is a place to start from."

"If you'll allow me to be blunt, John, that's nothing to start from. And if you'll allow me to be even blunter, all you've given me is that he's a queer dope user. Well, I guess that narrows it down a little."

"There's no need to be nasty," Stark said, and he seemed genuinely hurt.

"I'm not being nasty, I'm just making sure I've got the

facts since it seems some of them have only been implied and I don't want to work from the wrong implication."

Stark nodded. "You have the facts right."

I said nothing.

Miss Merton said, "So where will you start?" The color had come back into her face.

"I'll start with the crime blotters to make sure he wasn't picked up on a charge or thrown in the drunk tank or any other reason that the police might have gotten involved."

"I should have thought of that," Stark said.

"You wouldn't have gotten anywhere and might have caused yourself some embarrassment. I can call people I know and can keep your name out of it. If those calls are a washout, well, I suppose I can try Hub Gilplaine. He and I are old friends these days."

Stark nodded. He looked satisfied. "Potts can give you a check on the way out."

"Don't worry about it. I know you're good for it."

There was an awkward silence in which Stark looked out at his lawn, Miss Merton looked at her feet, and I watched the two of them.

"You're sure there's nothing more you can give me?" I said.

He shook his head.

"I'll call you when I've got something to report. It might not be today."

Stark looked up, shocked. "What if he's on the street?"

"It's warm out," I said. "You do understand, you've given me basically nothing to go on."

He returned his gaze to the horizon. "Of course," he said.

Miss Merton said, "We're all just so shaken by Mandy Ehrhardt's death."

Maybe she was and maybe she wasn't. Stark was shaken all right, and probably had cried all morning, but not over Mandy Ehrhardt.

I left them to commiserate, and let myself back into the house. The butler met me before I got out of the music room.

"Is there anything you require?" he said.

I didn't stop, and he fell in beside me. "Is Mr. Stark good friends with Miss Merton and her brother?" He didn't answer at first and I could see him try to think of a way to reply. I turned to him. We were in the main entrance. There were blinding patches of white on the marble floor in line with the windows. "Mr. Stark just hired me to find Greg Taylor. I think that he would want his staff to be cooperative, so that I can conduct my investigation."

The butler still hesitated, but said, "Yes, Mr. and Miss Merton are regular guests here. Their father, too. Many people from the studio are."

"They would all have known Mr. Taylor?"

"Yes."

"How about you? How well did you know Mr. Taylor?"

A disdainful expression came over his face. "We were hardly fraternal," the butler said.

"Of course," I said, and walked away from him, my shoes echoing in the hall.

THIRTEEN

I was just getting into my car when the front door opened again. "Mr. Foster!" Vera Merton ran on her tiptoes like a ballerina. "Wait."

I waited and she stopped short on the other side of the car. If she had been upset inside, she didn't show it now.

"Mr. Foster," she said, and then decided that she didn't like having the Packard between us. She came around to my side, the better to show me her legs. They were lovely legs. She could have been in pictures. Nobody would have complained about paying to look at her. She pulled at her lip and put her eyes in their corners so they weren't on me. Indecision didn't look natural on her.

"Am I supposed to guess what you want or are you going to tell me?"

"I just can't stop thinking about Mandy Ehrhardt," she said. "Do you have any ideas? About who did it?"

"I haven't been asked to have any. In fact, quite the opposite."

"How'd you come to find the—her?" Her eyes darted to my face and then went back to their corners.

"About the same way I found you and your brother yesterday. I just happened along at the wrong moment."

This time her eyes went right to mine. She tried to cover her nervousness with a smile. "So you weren't supposed to be, I don't know, following Mandy, or something?"

"Didn't you just get finished listening to Mr. Stark talk about how respectful I am of people's privacy?"

"Yes, but Daddy would want you to tell me. It's all right."

"If that's how he feels about it, he can tell me."

"Well, what were you doing at the studio yesterday?" she tried.

"I knew then, but I don't know now."

She pouted. "You're making this very difficult."

I gave her a knowing grin. "Sorry."

"I know that Daddy hired you yesterday and I know that you found Mandy's body. I'm just trying to understand." She paused for a second and decided she needed to add something to that. "It's all so horrible."

"Look, Miss Merton. I was hired by Al Knox, the head of security at the studio. If you want to take this up with Al, go ahead, but I've got work to do." To make it convincing, I should have gotten in my car, but I didn't.

She took a step closer and reached out to play with my tie. "You don't like me, is that it?"

We both watched her hand toy with the silk.

"You think my family are awful people."

"Miss Merton, I don't think of your family at all."

"Not even now?" She had found more inches to eliminate between us. Her perfume made me think of homemade cookies, which soured both her and the cookies.

"I'm trying harder to forget your family every minute."

"I just worry about Tommy. And Daddy," she said. "They need a woman around but all they've got is me, which isn't much of anything."

"You're definitely a woman."

She raised her head the right angle. "I knew you could say nice things."

"I can say all kinds of things."

"Why did Daddy hire you? Was it about Tommy? You can tell me."

"I told you before, your father didn't hire me, Al Knox did. If you think your father was behind it, you'd better go ask him. Whatever you and your brother do is no concern of mine. Though from what I've seen, your brother does altogether too much of whatever it is he does."

She stepped back then, all of her charm withdrawn. "How come you found Mandy?"

"It was an accident. It had nothing to do with anything."

"That's the best you can do?"

"I could do better, but you wouldn't like it."

She screwed herself up to say something more, but thought better of it and walked back to the house instead. She was a girl too used to getting what she wanted. Knox had warned me about her and her brother the day before, and now I could appreciate better what he'd meant. Poor Daddy. Running a movie studio wasn't all it was cracked up to be. You might give people orders, but that didn't mean your kids wouldn't run all over town getting into trouble. In fact, it probably ensured it.

I got into my car and rolled down the hill again. This missing person job seemed like only slightly more of a case than protecting Chloë Rose. It must have been my advertising: give me your money, no satisfaction guaranteed.

FOURTEEN

I was too close to the Rosenkrantz house to resist a visit. The way I figured it, I was owed the audience with Chloë Rose that I had been denied the night before. Knox may have thought that he could just throw me off of this thing, but the police wouldn't let me go that easily. With my name already in, it was for my own good that I meet the other person at the center of the storm. Anyway, Chloë Rose and Stark were co-stars, perhaps she knew Taylor, too.

Soso in mid-morning was a collection of geysers and waterfalls sprinkling the various lawns. It was the Rosenkrantzes' front lawn and flowerbeds that got the treatment this morning, requiring me to run a gauntlet to the front door. I timed it so I got the minimum shower. A faint shimmering rainbow appeared on the outer edge of the fan of water. It held a beautiful mystique, but collapsed before it could be properly admired, and then threatened to damage my suit a moment later.

I glanced back. There was a car parked out front. It was unmarked, but it said police anyway. It didn't fit with the neighborhood.

The door again opened before I could ring the bell. This time it was Detective Samuels and another plain-clothes cop. Miguel was visible beyond them, wringing his hands like an old maid.

"Don't you sleep, Foster?" Samuels said.

"No, I'm a vampire, didn't I tell you."

"Vampires can't go out during the day," the other cop said.

"Go on, you know all about it," I said.

The other cop looked away, embarrassed.

"I know you're not here about that murder," Samuels said. "Right?"

"You know, I heard a funny story about that," I said. "It had something to do with Chloë Rose being a suspect in your investigation. It was so ridiculous it made me laugh." I showed him how it made me laugh.

He was unimpressed. "This is a police investigation. You played it straight with me this morning, and I'm grateful for that. But I don't want any private dicks chasing my tail."

"And I'll do whatever I need to, to protect my client." If I could get her to be my client.

"Except provide her with an alibi. You still claim it wasn't a divorce job?"

"I don't do divorce."

Samuels cocked his head to his partner. "Come on, McEvoy. We've got work."

They waited for the sprinkler to finish its cycle, and then hurried down the wet path to their car.

Miguel came forward to stand in the doorframe. He greeted me like a long-lost cousin, stopping just short of giving me a hug. "That was the police," he said.

"I hadn't noticed. Were any others here?"

He shook his head. "No, just those two."

"When did they get here?"

"Maybe an hour ago. Maybe a little more. They talked to both Mr. Rosenkrantz and Miss Rose."

"About what?" I said.

He averted his eyes. "I wouldn't know. They were private conversations."

"You can skip that bit. What did they say?"

He bobbed his head to show his reluctance, but then opened up as though he couldn't wait to tell somebody. "About a murder. Another actress in Miss Rose's movie was killed. They asked Mr. Rosenkrantz about his relationship with this actress, when he had seen her last, did she have any enemies, was she afraid of anything."

"Sure, I know the drill. And Miss Rose?"

He shook his head. "They kept asking her where she was last night. They would talk about something else, and then they would ask her again if she was sure she had been here the whole time, and had she made any phone calls, and had nobody seen her? She got very upset. She had to lie down. What about you, Mr. Foster? Where were you last night?"

"Out gambling. Where can I find Miss Rose?"

He waited. I started around him. He thought about trying to stop me, but it was only a thought. Instead he led the way. We took the squared arch to the right, entering a dining room with a heavy wooden baroque dining set. We went through a door on the opposite side into a poorly lit antechamber in which hung a portrait daguerreotype of a cat. This opened into the library, which was arranged like a sitting room with Louis XV loveseats facing each other over a delicate Chippendale table. The fireplace was large enough to stand in, but it didn't look like it had been used anytime during the current administration. The built-in shelves housed richly bound volumes in matching sets. Everything in the room looked like it belonged in a museum.

Chloë Rose was on the loveseat facing the entryway when I came in. If Vera Merton was one kind of woman, then this was the other. She had the kind of beauty that made you nervous you were going to do something that would break it. She wore no makeup, and her eyes were red from crying. She had on a simple navy ankle-length skirt and a white-on-white patterned blouse.

I took off my hat, and gave her a moment to collect herself.

"Your colleagues were just here," she said. Her accent was faint but it was there.

"I'm not the police, Miss Rose. I'm the private investigator that was hired to protect you yesterday." I got out one of my cards. She made no motion to take it, so I left it for her on the corner of the table.

"So you know," she said.

"I found the body."

Her tears threatened to fall again, but she held them back. "They said you were supposed to be here last night. It seems that the fact that you weren't is not in my favor just now."

"No, it's not," I said.

"Shem and Mandy were sleeping together. It wasn't any secret. Everyone knew."

"It didn't bother you?"

She looked at me with eyes that were suddenly indignant. "Of course it did. It killed me. But what could I do?"

"You could have left him."

"Oh, it's so easy for a stranger to stand there and say I should have left him. You come in and you know: leave him!"

"I didn't say you should have, I said you could have. And I didn't say it was easy."

She collapsed back on the loveseat again. "What does it matter? Mandy killed. Why does any of it matter?"

"I hope that's not what you told the police," I said.

She shook her head, her voice growing pinched again. "No. They just wanted to know where I had been, over and over. I said here. But I can't prove it. I'm a suspect in a murder. Oh, God! I thought I was finished with the police. Finished with prisons, finished with the police, a new life here in the saint's city."

She sounded as though she was just barely keeping hysteria at bay. I remembered Al Knox's original description. And now I could see the capacity for panic, for melancholy. I took a step forward, but resisted the urge to put a hand on her shoulder. "You're not going to be arrested. We just need to figure out what really happened. Then you'll be in the clear."

She looked up at me and it was almost as though she noticed me for the first time. "Mr. Foster? What do you want? What are you doing here?"

"Protecting myself as much as you. The studio fired me this morning. I don't know which of us is being set up here, or maybe it's both of us, but I needed to talk to you before figuring out what to do next."

She looked frightened. "I don't know what you're talking about."

"Don't worry," I said. "That's my job, not yours. Can you tell me what's this about prisons, and police? Is it connected to something that happened to you in France...?"

I thought she was going to start crying again, but the spell had passed. Now her delivery was cold, her accent heavier than when she had been taking pains to control it. "My father was a safecracker." She rubbed the heel of one palm against her eyes as she spoke, first the left, then the right. "He was killed in prison many years ago."

"The police questioned you about his death?"

She turned her look on me. "It was many years ago."

All the same, I could see how it could play into Samuels' circumstantial case, if she'd been questioned once about another murder. But I didn't say anything about that to her. "There's nothing you could do to document your time last night?"

"I was asleep in bed," she said.

"Your husband's son? He's staying with you, isn't he?"

"Shem sent him back east yesterday afternoon, before all of this."

"The neighbors, then? Maybe they could confirm you never went out."

"They could say they saw my car still here, but there was enough traffic on the street last night, no one could say I didn't get a ride. Anyway, our nearest neighbors were out late to a gala."

It was still all circumstantial. They didn't have the murder weapon, they couldn't have her prints in Ehrhardt's house, and they didn't have a witness. But people went to jail on circumstantial evidence. They certainly went to trial.

I had another idea. "Let's go back to the man you thought was following you. Was Miss Ehrhardt always there too, when you saw him? You told Al it was usually on the studio lot, right?"

She looked frightened and the pitch of her voice went up. "Why does that matter?"

"Because maybe the man following you was also following her."

She knitted her brow in thought, shaking her head back and forth. "I couldn't say, not for sure. Probably yes, she was there, but…" Back and forth, back and forth. "I don't know about at the first fitting. And I thought there might be someone following my car once or twice; I was alone then." The memory seemed to trouble her. Her eyes were wide now with fear. She shook her head even faster.

"Miss Rose?"

She sat up rigid. "No, it couldn't be that he was following Mandy. He's following me."

"Don't get excited."

"No, no, no."

I reached for her, but before I could get to her Miguel was there with a drink on a tray. "Try this, Miss Rose. Try this."

He managed to get the glass into her hand, and she raised it mechanically, still shaking her head. The liquor went in, she shuddered, and fell back. Miguel grabbed the glass from her hand before the last sip could spill. He looked at me, imploring, and then left the room with the tray tucked under his arm and the glass in his hand.

"You don't have more on the description of that man," I said, a fighter kicking his opponent when he's down.

She said nothing.

"Okey," I said. "I'll show myself out."

That didn't get any reaction either. She just lay there, collapsed, her beautiful face miserable in a way that the public never got to see on screen. It was disconcerting, like seeing the skull beneath the skin.

I made my way back to the front hall. Miguel was waiting for me.

"You see how fragile Miss Rose is?"

"Yeah, I see. Did she pull the same act with the police?"

"Nearly."

"Samuels can't want her for this. He'd see right away she's no good for it. Unless he tries to play her as crazy." It was my turn to shake my head. "Listen, I didn't get a chance to ask Miss Rose. Are she and John Stark close? Would she know his friends?"

"Not that I know of. Miss Rose keeps to herself."

I nodded. "Thanks." I put on my hat and took a step towards the door. "Call me if there's an emergency. I'm not wanted here otherwise."

"Actually, Mr. Rosenkrantz would like to see you."

I turned back. "And how would Mr. Rosenkrantz know I was here?"

"He saw you come in." He indicated the stairs and said, "If you'll allow me."

I thought about how it was really not my business. I thought about how little I had to go on. I thought about how the studio and the police had told me to clear out and stay clear.

"Lead the way," I said.

FIFTEEN

The room was supposed to be a study, but the same person who decorated Hub Gilplaine's office had decorated this room too. Every visible surface except for a small path from the door to the desk was covered in books and papers. There were unfinished shelves screwed into the length of one wall, bowing under the weight of the books piled on them. One shelf had ripped out of the wall and fallen onto the books on the shelf beneath it. That one only held because of the piles of books on the floor propping it up from below. The papers were strewn about in inelegant stacks, the edges curling. There appeared to be a green imitation-leather easy chair in one of the corners, but there was no way to get to it now. By comparison, the surface of the desk was relatively tidy, dominated as it was by an Underwood typewriter. There was a bottle of vodka that had had a good deal of its contents acquainted with a glass, and an already empty bottle on the floor beside the desk chair. The place smelled of alcohol and old paper.

Rosenkrantz turned to face me. He looked pale and his eyes were dilated, but he had no trouble sitting up straight or tracking me. When he spoke, it was surprisingly clear, the sign of a practiced drinker. "You followed me from the Carrot-Top," he said.

It didn't require an answer so I didn't give him one.

"You saw what they did…"

"What who did?" I said.

"This goddamn life. This goddamn city. These goddamn people."

For a great writer, he seemed awfully hung up on one word. "Had she any enemies?" I asked.

He looked up again. "What are you, the police? They were already here."

"Okey. Then what did you want to see me about?"

"They say Clotilde did it."

"They do."

"She didn't."

"I know."

He nodded, satisfied with the work that had been done so far. We had who didn't do it established beyond a doubt. He shook his head as he reached for the bottle and brought it to the rim of his empty glass. He didn't have any trouble with the maneuver. "Mandy didn't have any enemies. No one she'd fought with. Nobody she was scared of. Nobody who cared either way."

"Friends?"

"I know that she made friends with a few of the girls that worked in the club where she was waitressing, but just to go out and have a laugh with. Maybe some of the valets too. She was new to San Angelo."

"And the name of the club?"

He lowered his head and looked at me out of the tops of his eyes.

"The Carrot-Top."

"No, but close enough. The Tip. That's where I met her."

"You said you could put her in movies."

He shrugged, raising his glass in a toast. "And I actually did." He drank the whole thing down in two gulps.

"I guess there's a first for everything," I said.

He raised his empty glass again. "Hear, hear."

"Well this is lots of fun. You could probably charge a door fee. You might need to share the alcohol though."

"She was a swell kid, Foster. I didn't love her. In fact we fought just as much as we laughed. But she could really lay into you, and always made it good afterward. She was a swell kid."

"Sure. And she had a heart of gold. And she never would hurt a fly."

His face clouded and he looked up at me. "Ah, go to hell." He grabbed the bottle for a refill.

"Should I send Miguel up with another bottle?"

"Why weren't you here last night doing your job!"

"I know my place," I said. "I know I'm not supposed to say, why weren't you here with your wife, or why weren't you at Miss Ehrhardt's place to protect her. Because if we always ask ourselves why then pretty soon we can make anything our fault."

"Especially when it is."

I nodded. "Then too."

He sneered and shook his head. "God, the people in this town will cut your throat and tell you they're giving you a shave. They're not people, even. They're money, with no eyes and no heart, or they're raw desire hidden behind bulletproof glass. You can see them, but you can't touch them. Either you go through the system until you're just money, too, or you find out that your bulletproof glass wasn't as bulletproof as advertised. If at any point you remember you're a person, you better watch out, you're halfway on the bus home."

"I hate to interrupt the great American man of letters while he's being insightful, but you'll have to excuse me."

"You'll go and talk to Hub now, won't you?"

"I'm no longer working this case."

"That's why you came here. Because you're no longer working on it."

"Just some matters I wanted to tie up."

He considered me for a moment. "When you go see Hub, ask him about Janice Stoneman." He waited for me to write it down. I didn't. He refilled his glass and downed it without preliminaries, then sat staring at it. "Huh." He looked up from his empty glass. "In my books, the characters always have a moment of realization, some object or event that crystallizes their very being. Not the trash I write for Gilplaine, my real books. But who really recognizes the moment that his life changes? At the time, I mean. Maybe later, but not at the time." He shook his head and sighed. "I was wrong, what I told you a minute ago. It would be bad enough if it was those Hollywood bastards that cut your throat. But no, you cut your own throat. Up until the moment it's done, it's not done, but once it is done…" He opened his hand in front of him as though letting a lightning bug go.

"Tell Hub I don't ever want to see him again." He picked up the bottle, but I didn't wait for him to refill his glass.

Downstairs, there was no sign of Miguel. Miss Rose must have required his further assistance. If I'd been smart, I would have counted myself lucky that my own assistance was no longer required. But like the man said, you don't know you're holding the razor until after it's too late.

SIXTEEN

It was a little after noon. The Tip served lunch, but Gilplaine probably didn't come in until mid-afternoon; part of his job was to be seen by the night people. I stopped at the lunch counter in the hotel across from the Blackstone and had a melted cheese sandwich with a slice of bacon as its backbone. The coffee had grounds in it, but I drank it anyway. The mid-day paper was out and there was now a small piece buried on the last page of section one, no more than four inches, about a waitress killed in Harbor City. I wondered how Rosenkrantz would take that. They cut your throat even after they've cut your throat.

Back in my office, I picked up the phone while walking around the desk to my chair. There were any number of cops I could call to look over the morning report for me, some who might even do it. But if I was going to end up in Harbor City again, it was best to maintain good relations. Samuels picked up on the third ring. "Shouldn't you be out investigating something?"

"Who's this?"

"Foster. I was wondering if you could give me a little information."

"Try the operator. I'm busy."

"You get a chance to glance over the morning report? It's out already, isn't it?"

"You think I have time for that kind of thing? I'm working a murder. What are you doing? I told you to cool it."

"New case. Missing person. Wanted to relieve you of any concern about my intentions with regard to your murder."

"Okey, funny man. You've got five minutes. Who you looking for?"

"Name's Greg Taylor. Blonde male, clean-shaven, early to mid twenties, last seen wearing pale blue pants and a white shirt with no jacket or tie. Real pretty boy."

A moment passed while Samuels flipped through the list of the night's crimes. After a minute, he said, "Nothing. No luck. Now is there anything else I can get you, your majesty?"

"No, that's about what I expected. Thanks, Samuels, call me if you need me."

He hung up without a reply. It was good for him to think that I owed him something. He'd be more likely to keep me informed that way. I checked my watch. Just after one. It was still a little early for Gilplaine to be at the Tip. I found a rag stuffed in the back of one of my file cabinets and gave the office the once over. It probably only kicked up more dust, giving it a chance to redistribute, but at least I didn't feel as much like an embarrassment to my profession. I threw the rag back where it had been hiding. I couldn't think of any other stalls, so I locked up the office and headed for the Tip. If Gilplaine wasn't there yet, I could at least feel out the other employees without his interference. It was the best lead I had.

The lunch crowd at the Tip was just finishing. Still, everyone looked up when I came in, to make sure I wasn't someone important. I wasn't.

The room was smaller than it looked in the newspapers. There were maybe twenty circular tables in the center of the room around the fountain. Some were large enough only for two, some for up to four. They were each draped with two tablecloths, one white that hung to the floor, the other small and black that hung over the edge of the table just enough to form isosceles triangles at each place setting. The tables were bunched close together, with hardly enough room for the tuxedoed wait staff to fit between the patrons' chairs. There were circular booths lining the two outer walls, four to a side, and a staircase just inside the door led to an open balcony with three more booths that had a view of the whole room. The centerpiece was the fountain, an imitation Roman marble with Cupid sitting at Aphrodite's feet, shooting a plume of water from his bow and arrow into the well below. Or maybe it wasn't an imitation. I wasn't an expert on Roman statues.

All of the tables were filled. The noise was distracting. The kitchen was in the back, and there was another door in the back wall labeled *Private*.

The maître d' was a thin man in his late fifties. He combed his scant hair over his balding crown for the maximum effect. He unwisely sported a Hitler mustache, and both the mustache and the remaining hair were pitch black. He adjusted the leather reservation book on the podium in front of him with both hands and looked at me down his nose with borrowed superiority.

"Do you have a reservation, sir?"

"I'm not here to eat," I said.

There was a spark of recognition in his eyes. "Of course not, sir. Police, then."

"Private. Work here long?"

"Only six months, sir. I used to be at the Haviland on Seventh. May I ask what this is regarding?"

"Do you know Mandy Ehrhardt?"

"Should I, sir?"

"You can stow the sir, and stop answering my questions with questions. She used to work here."

"No," he said, pausing to pretend to think about it, "I don't believe I know anybody by that name. Now you'll have to tell me what this is about or I'm afraid I'll have to ask you to leave. This is a private establishment."

"Yeah, private. Where everyone can see everyone." I handed him my card. "I want to see Gilplaine."

The maître d' sucked in his lips and held my card away from him by its edges. "Mr. Gilplaine is not here at the moment."

I had expected Gilplaine would be out, but I recognized that 'not here at the moment.' Not here for *me*. I pushed. "Why don't you show him the card and let him decide if he's in or not?"

He seemed to be deciding whether it would be safe to throw me out or if I actually had some pull with the boss.

"And tell him I expect to get that card back. He already has one, and they cost."

"Yes, *sir*," he said.

He turned on his heel and crossed the room to the aisle that ran along the booths on the right, then went through the door marked *Private*. Nothing happened except for servers trailing in and out of the kitchen, giving quick glances of a white well-lit place through the swinging door. The noise in the restaurant remained constant. It didn't matter what anyone was saying; it all sounded the same. Cupid's stream was never-ending.

It was no more than two minutes before the maître d' appeared again, walking quickly towards the front with an excellent display of good posture. When he regained his place at the podium, he said, "Mr. Gilplaine will see you in his office. Take the door by the kitchen, and you'll see his office at the end of the hall."

"It's a good thing that Mr. Gilplaine just got back in time to see me," I said.

No one looked at me as I crossed the room. The door marked *Private* led to a small corridor, no more than ten feet with two doors to the left and one straight ahead. That door was open. Gilplaine was behind a desk that could have been a twin of the one at the Carrot-Top Club, but the desk was the only thing about it that resembled the office at the casino. This was a pristine environment with no boxes piled up and nothing on the desk other than a bronze souvenir ashtray from Tijuana, two black telephones, and a small clock that was turned to face Gilplaine. There was another desk in the corner, a smaller metal one with a typewriter on it and two neat stacks of paper. The walls were hung with framed photographs of Gilplaine with one movie star or another. They were all autographed as well. Leaning up against one wall was the big boy from the night before, grinning like I was a long-lost friend.

I came in and closed the door behind me.

"You have one minute to say something interesting," Gilplaine said.

"Interesting to who?"

Instead of answering, he turned the clock on his desk so that we could both see the thin red second hand sweep around the dial.

"I'm looking for Greg Taylor," I said. There was no reaction at all. "I was told he comes here. I thought maybe you or someone on your staff—"

"I won't have my staff harassed by some snoop who's decided to pester me."

"If you call this pestering, I'd like to see what you consider being friendly."

"Your minute's going fast, Foster."

"This guy is young, early twenties with sandy blonde hair and fine features. He's just the kind of pretty boy that makes the queers go gaga when he bats his lashes. He hangs out with movie people."

Gilplaine sat back in his chair. "Whatever game you're playing, you can stop it."

"This isn't a game. I call this work."

"What's it have to do with Chloë Rose?"

"I didn't say it had anything to do with Chloë Rose."

"So you haven't come to ask me about Mandy Ehrhardt's death?"

"I'm no longer involved with the Rose case, and Mandy Ehrhardt's something else altogether."

"You just found the body."

I said nothing to that. I certainly didn't ask him how he knew. A man like Gilplaine had a way of knowing things.

He and the police were best friends. Drinks on the house anytime.

"Edwards said you asked him about Mandy," he said.

"He also said you weren't here. I don't think his word is to be trusted. Anyway, I told you, it's not the same case."

He turned his clock back to face him. "Time's up, friend."

"I'd like to ask your bartender whether Taylor was in last night or not."

"The police already wasted an hour of his time. That's like wasting an hour of mine."

"The cops came here?" I said. "Did you forget a payment or does your arrangement with them not cover Harbor City murders?"

He snapped his fingers over his shoulder and said, "Mitch." His man came off the wall and stepped forward.

I stepped back. "Okey. I'm going."

Gilplaine watched me as I stepped back again, my hand now on the door handle. His expression was the same one the tiger gives you at the zoo: forlorn frustration that he was prevented from ripping you limb from limb.

He had given me nothing when I had asked for little more. It was out of a need to strike back that I said, with one foot on the threshold, "Just out of curiosity. What can you tell me about Janice Stoneman?"

His eyes narrowed at that, his lower jaw jutting out from under his upper. I like to throw peanuts at the tigers too. "Who?" he said.

"I thought maybe she worked for you. Like Mandy. I haven't started asking around yet, but if she did, I'm sure people will remember—"

His expression grew more thoughtful. "Did you say Janice?" he said. He smiled widely, showing off his dental work. "We did have a Janice working here some time ago. Haven't seen her for months, since December at least. She had to go back to her folks in Kansas or Oklahoma or one of those places these girls come from. We owed her some money. Tried to get it to her, but with no luck. Is that what this Taylor business is about? I'd love a chance to get Janice her money."

I had been shooting in the dark. I never expected him to get loquacious. I kept playing it by ear. "When did you say you saw her last? There's some confusion about the date she left. Some say it was at the beginning of December, some say the beginning of January. The police aren't much better."

"Who'd you talk to at the police?" he asked through his smile, which wasn't so wide anymore.

"You'll understand, I can't say."

"I think it was just before Christmas," he said. "I seem to recall she was going home for the holidays." He shrugged and frowned. "Never came back."

I nodded as though that meant something to me. "You know, it's kind of funny, two women who worked for you, and one's dead and the other's missing."

He couldn't keep up his smile through that. "Who said she's missing? Just because I couldn't find her."

"I'd think you'd be able to find anyone you wanted."

He shook his head. "These kids come through here. They work a few weeks, a month, it's always temporary. If a couple of them disappear, wind up in bad situations, well, that's just what happens. It's San Angelo."

"It is San Angelo." The subject appeared to be exhausted. Mitch, meanwhile, looked ready to go nine rounds. I turned to go.

"This Taylor," Gilplaine said, slowly, as if just remembering. "Is he a junky? Hangs out with John Stark?"

I didn't say anything.

His smile came back, as comforting as the Cheshire cat's. "A lot might go on in my clubs, but not the sort of thing you're thinking about. Not what this Taylor kid was after. I suggest you go down to Market Street in Harbor City. You might do better there."

"I thought you didn't know him."

He shook his head a little bit yes and a little bit no. "I know a lot of people. I can't always remember all of them."

"Sure," I said, "you have a memory like a goldfish." I nodded to both men and shut the door behind me.

At the maître d' stand, I asked Edwards, "Were you on the door last night?"

He shifted his weight.

"Oh, come on, you can tell me that much. I could find it out from almost anybody."

He looked behind him as though the answer would be there. He was no gangster, just a dandified waiter.

"Look," I said. "I was just making conversation before. This is serious."

"Yes, I was on the door."

"And did you see a young blonde man, very slight build, medium height, maybe high on heroin?"

"No I did not," he said in a way that made it clear that he regretted saying anything and that he wouldn't say anything else.

"Thank you," I said, and left the club. I got in my car and sat for a moment behind the wheel. Gilplaine literally wouldn't give me the time of day when he thought I was looking into Mandy Ehrhardt's murder, and Taylor meant even less to him, though he did know who he was. But when I added Janice Stoneman in, he was quick to give me an answer that would keep me satisfied and working on something else. I sat for five minutes thinking, maybe ten. There was nothing more to do on Taylor until Market Street opened for the night. I started the engine. As I eased away from the curb, a sand-colored coupe pulled out of an alley along the side of the club and fell in behind me. Gilplaine was telling me too much.

SEVENTEEN

The main branch of the San Angelo Public Library was in an art deco building that had been built by workers in the W.P.A. Its façade made gestures towards grandeur, but inside it wasn't much more than a warehouse. The coupe parked half a block behind me, but I wasn't too worried that one of Gilplaine's men would take a step into a library.

I went to the periodical department and got out the bound volume of the *S.A. Times* for last December. I scanned all the way through the paper from December 20 onward, including every advertisement and job posting. I found nothing of interest the first three days. Then I started on the issue for December 23. It was at the bottom of page three. They probably hadn't wanted to spoil anyone's Christmas; otherwise it would have been a front-page piece. An unidentified woman's remains had been found on the beach in Harbor City. Her throat had been slit and her thighs had been gashed open. I flipped through the next few days' papers. The story moved to page six on December 24 and wasn't mentioned again after that. The woman still hadn't been identified as of Christmas Eve. Clearly Gilplaine thought that it had been Janice Stoneman.

I placed my hand on the fold in the page and looked around. There were only a few other men in the room, all engrossed in their reading. I coughed and tore the article out. I returned the volume to the periodicals clerk and started for the front door, but stopped just before going out. As long as I was here, I might as well look into everything.

I went to the circulation desk. A plump woman wearing a lily-patterned tea-length skirt over a pink silk blouse smiled as I came up. She had prematurely silver hair streaked with white, which she had braided and wrapped around her head like a coronet, holding the whole thing in place with a box worth of bobby pins. Half-lens reading glasses hung from a cord around her neck, but she hadn't been using them to consult the volume opened flat on the counter in front of her. It looked like a dictionary.

"May I help you?" she said.

"Yes," I said. "I'd like to find some information about a horse called…" I pulled out the sheet I'd torn from the notepad in the Rosenkrantz home the night before. "Constant Comfort," I said.

The librarian frowned. "I don't approve of horseracing. I voted no in that election."

"I did too. Horseracing is dreadful and only dirty and dangerous people go in for it. This isn't about racing. A friend of mine just got this horse, but he thinks he might have been cheated. He just wants to see who owned it before him to make sure he got the right one."

"I'm sure I don't know about that. Would City Hall keep those kinds of records?"

"I don't know. That's why I asked you."

"I'm sorry, I have no idea." She pulled her lips in,

causing little wrinkles to erupt around her mouth. Those were premature too.

I knocked on the counter twice. "You know what? Never mind. Thank you for your help."

So much for Constant Comfort.

I went outside. A bank of phone booths stood against the wall of the building. A broad-shouldered man in a navy blue suit and no hat leaned against the nearest booth. His hair was slicked back and his brown brogues were freshly polished. But he wasn't there for me. He held a racing form folded into a rigid rectangle about the size of a closed street map, in case anyone might be confused about what he was doing there. He looked up at me as I came down the steps, then looked back at his paper when he saw that I wasn't a customer. I went into the booth furthest from his, and pulled the door shut. The overhead light turned on and the exhaust fan in the ceiling began whirring. It didn't help. The booth was still stifling.

I dropped a coin in the slot and dialed. It was answered after one ring. "*Chronicle*."

"Pauly Fisher, please."

The line began to hum, and then there was a click, and then Pauly's warm voice came on. "Fisher here."

"It's Dennis Foster."

"Foster. What you got for me?"

I cracked the door just enough to get some air. "Maybe something. Maybe nothing. You remember a murder in Harbor City just before Christmas? Jane Doe, slit throat, carved-up legs?"

"Maybe. I don't know. What about it?"

"You only get the news that's in the paper or do you get the real stuff?" I wiped the back of my neck with my handkerchief.

"What? You're thinking of this starlet that got herself cut up yesterday?"

"Sounds like they were cut up in the same ways."

"Sounds like a coincidence to me."

"Well, can we find out if it's been a coincidence any other times?"

"You must be kidding."

"What?"

"You know what I'd have to go through to find that out? I hope you don't need it this week."

I tried to entice him. "I think I've got a name for Jane Doe."

"Nobody came looking for her. It's not news."

"Don't you find that odd? You'd agree that a cut throat and carved-up legs normally is news, right? Especially when it's a nice-looking young woman on the receiving end."

"Yeah."

"Then why was it buried on page three? And a dead story two days later?" I heard the faint electric whistle along the phone line that passed for silence. Now I had caught his interest. I sweetened it. "What if it wasn't a coincidence? What if there were other women?"

"You been reading about Jack the Ripper again?"

I waited.

He sighed. "Okey. But it's going to take me a while."

"Try my office first. If I'm not there, try the apartment.

Oh, and Pauly, one more thing, do you know anything about a horse named Constant Comfort?"

"I know about horses as much as I know about Einstein."

"All right. Thanks." I hung up. I opened the door and stepped out of the phone booth. There was one man around here who'd know more about horses than about Einstein. He was in the same spot I had left him, still holding his little folded racing form. I walked down the bank of booths.

He saw me coming and he tucked the paper under his arm and held out his hands, palms up. "I'm just waiting on a call from my aunt to tell me my uncle's out of the hospital."

"What's he in for?"

The man readjusted his stance. "Appendicitis."

"Next time try he was in a car wreck. Sounds better."

He tilted his head and squinted.

"I'm not a cop," I said. I held up a five-dollar bill. "What do you know about a horse named Constant Comfort?"

"You're sure you're not a cop?"

I crinkled the money. "Private."

He checked to see if he needed a shave. He did. He probably needed to shave after every meal. "Comfort doesn't race anymore. He won a couple of pots last year. Out to pasture now."

"You know who owns him?"

"He was in Daniel Merton's stable when he was racing. I don't know about now. Why? You in the market for a horse?"

"Nah, your horse might have appendicitis."

I held out the bill to him, and he snatched it away as though he expected me to do the same. He pocketed it and made a big production of taking the racing form out from under his arm and finding his place. He leaned back against the booth again, but his eyes weren't moving across the page. He was waiting for me to leave.

At the curb I got back in my Packard. Daniel Merton was one of the founders and owners, and the current president, of Merton Stein Productions. If he had owned the horse before and Chloë Rose owned it now, he must have given it to her. But he was also the man she worked for, which made him the one the mystery man on the phone had been calling on behalf of. Why would Merton want to buy back a horse he'd given her?

I started the engine. None of this was my business. I had a client, and he probably expected me to work for my money.

I checked the time. Almost five. It was too early for any of the right people to be on Market Street in Harbor City and too late to go sit around the office. I decided to go home, and wait for Pauly Fisher's phone call. The sand-colored coupe decided to join me.

EIGHTEEN

I didn't bother locking my apartment door. If Hub's men wanted to get in, they'd get in, the only question was whether I'd have to deal with a busted doorframe afterwards.

I took up a position so I'd be behind the door when it opened. I stood there and nothing happened. I kept standing, feeling like a fool. But in the last thirty-six hours I'd had a gun pointed at me, been threatened by gangsters and by the police, and found a mutilated body. I waited.

The knock came, three heavy thuds made with the meat of a fist. I stayed quiet. We all listened to the floorboards. The knock again, more insistent, and this time, "Come on, Foster. We know you're in there. We just want to talk." It was Mitch's voice.

I heard a hand on the doorknob, and then the door swung towards me, but faster and harder than I'd expected. It slammed into my hip, sending a sharp pain up and down my side. I must have cried out, because Mitch hurled his full weight against the door, pinning me behind it. I tried to lean forward but my shoulders were pushed together, my arms in front of me like a fighter trying to protect his middle. I was stuck.

Mitch peeked around the door, still holding his weight against it. At the sight of me, he eased the pressure for a moment only to fall back against the door, shooting pain along my shoulder blades.

A second man appeared, rail thin and well over six feet tall, wearing a gray suit with a black vest underneath. He patted me down to see if I had a gun. I didn't. He took the newspaper article I'd stolen from the library out of my pocket. Then he nodded at Mitch.

The weight fell away from the door and I staggered forward. "What do you two want?"

The tall man unfolded the newspaper article, glanced it over, and looked back at me. "For somebody not working on a murder, you have an interesting choice of reading material."

"I just ripped that out for the crossword on the back."

He held up the backside, which wasn't a crossword. "We were told to give you a chance. We were told to use our discretion."

"I told it to Gilplaine straight. I'm working another job."

"Then how do you explain this?"

I couldn't explain it. I couldn't even say why it was important. I didn't know anything other than I was a damn fool for having gotten mixed up with this business in the first place.

"Mr. Gilplaine finds your explanation unconvincing," the tall man said. He turned to Mitch, who was jumping lightly in place on the balls of his feet, like he was warming up. "Leave his face alone. This is only a warning."

I tried to dodge to my left in an attempt to get out the door, but Mitch barreled into me, slamming me back up against it. Holding me there, he punched me in the kidney.

One would have been plenty, but he did it again and then a third time, so that my legs went watery and tears pushed out between my squinting eyelids. A fire lapped around my midsection. He let me go since he was sure I wasn't going anywhere now. Before I could collapse, he propped me up and punched me just once in the stomach. I doubled over, throwing my upper torso into Mitch's waiting fist. The dull ache of my pectoral met up with the fire in my side, and I fell back against the door, trying to draw breath and failing.

Mitch stood up, his breathing only slightly heavy. "He doesn't look too good, does he?"

The tall man made no comment. We could have been reading the stock prices. He was bored.

Mitch jumped in place again. "I think I better even him out." He twisted his torso, bringing his arm all the way back. He was going to show me that fist long before it was going to get to me. I couldn't move anyway, and he barreled it into my other kidney. I fell forward onto my knees.

"He's blocking the door."

"You're in the way," Mitch said. He shoved me over with the toe of one shoe. I didn't resist. I couldn't have if I'd tried.

"I think we've made our point," the tall man said.

Mitch kicked me in the stomach once more for good measure. Before I could catch my breath, he bent down and snaked a thick arm around my windpipe, his hot breath up against my ear. "Just because I'm not supposed to mark up your face don't mean I've got to leave you conscious, you flatfooted…"

Whatever it was that he called me was lost to the ages.

There were more interesting things to command my attention, black splotches appearing before my eyes intermixed with white flashes, and then the black beat out the white and then I was drifting above the floor, high up near the ceiling, and then I wasn't.

The black-and-white flicker of a movie screen came on in front of me, the test strip counting down five, four, three, two, one. Chloë Rose lit up the screen, a radiant aura around her. There were quick cuts and there was a knife and there was a gun, and then there was a body floating on a pool of blood. Chloë Rose came back again, and she was screaming. She was beautiful. Then there was a man seen from behind. It must have been the star of the picture. John Stark or Hub Gilplaine. He came to a mirror and I saw that it was me. But I'm down there with the paying marks in the cinema seats. How could I be up on the screen? The image flickered past. There was a lanky brunette stuffing a body into a car. There was another body floating in a pool of blood, but this time the blood was mixed with white foam. It was on the beach, and the waves were lapping away at the black blood, white, black, white, black, a gaping throat. A gunshot. And they're off. The horses pounded around the track. Cut to the stands. Chloë Rose. The horses rounding the far turn. Cut to the stands. Mitch and the tall man and me holding our tickets. The horses are coming around. Cut to the stands. John Stark holding hands with Greg Taylor. The photoflash! It hurts my eyes. And then the horse race was a prize fight and Mitch was in the ring with me and the bell was being rung...

❋

And then suddenly it was a telephone ringing.

A voice said, "Turn off the lights."

I took a deep breath and immediately started coughing. Every part of my upper torso ached, except when I moved, at which point the ache was replaced with shooting pain.

"It's too bright," the voice said. "Turn off the light and bring me a drink."

No one answered, and it's a good thing, because I was alone.

I looked over at the phone, but it had stopped ringing. If it ever had been ringing. Maybe it had just been my head.

I put my hand against the wall. It was a good wall. It stayed where you left it. Not like my breath. I gasped to draw it in, my throat getting tight, but in it went, and I exhaled with the only consequence being more throbbing and jabbing along my ribs.

The wall helped me to my knees and even held me when I fell against it. Like I said, it was a good wall. I was able to reach up and flip off the light.

Now it was too dark. Whatever little light was supposed to come from the window in the bathroom wasn't there, so I'd been out at least a couple of hours.

Okey, Foster, one step at a time. That's the way. Hands and knees. Now just knees. What do you say about feet?

One foot was under me now, and then with the help of the doorknob I got up onto both feet and stumbled across to my chair and fell into it. The newspaper article was sitting on the bed. That was nice of them. They were solid people who wouldn't steal a newspaper clipping from an unconscious man. The library should hire those two. They'd never have any late returns again.

I rested for some amount of time, relearning how to breathe. I got so I was pretty good at it. I could even do it with my eyes closed. When I had gotten that under my belt, I figured I might as well try for that drink. I got to my feet, and this time it wasn't like riding a bicycle with a bent wheel. I made it to the liquor, poured a stiff drink, and drank it off in one gulp, enjoying the only burning inside of me that I had put there. While I poured another one, the phone began to ring again. Or maybe it was the first time. I looked at it way over on the side table. It was probably Pauly Fisher. Anything he had to tell me, I didn't want to know just then; he could call me at the office tomorrow.

I made my way back to the light switch with the second drink in my hand, the phone still ringing. The lights came on and I squinted, holding up my hand as if to ward off a blow.

I drank the second drink. I could see then. The clock on my nightstand said it was almost half past eight. It had been just about five when I'd left the library. I'd been out for three hours, assuming it wasn't the next day.

The phone was still hollering at anyone who would listen. Pauly Fisher wasn't that persistent, but I didn't want to find out who was. It was still plenty early for Market Street—in fact, it might still have been too early. But it was time to go either way. Because that was my job. All of this other stuff was just a sideline, a hobby.

I looked at the newspaper article again. Gilplaine had

done me a favor in his own vicious way. He'd told me this dead woman was much more important than I'd known. That seemed like a mistake a man like Gilplaine wouldn't make. Maybe someday I'd know why.

I thought about a third drink, but left my glass on the table and went to the door instead. I got it open without any problem. No one was waiting outside. It was just me and the hallway. They seemed pretty confident I'd gotten the message. I'd gotten it, but it might not have been the message they intended.

I locked up behind me and leaned against the wall. Behind my door the telephone was still ringing. That was an awfully long time to let a phone ring. Maybe it was important after all.

But getting out of there was important too. Whoever it was could call back.

I went down the hall, took the automatic elevator, and found my car just like a man who had all of his organs in the right place.

NINETEEN

Market Street in Harbor City meant Market Street between Fifth and Sixth, a rundown block of seedy bars that had been glamorous at some time but no one could remember when. Among the fairies it was known simply as The Market. If you were a pretty boy on the prowl, The Market would be one of the first places you would go. In its heyday, neon signs and flashing lights had gone up all along the length of the block, and the signs had survived the block's decline, making for a rather bright underworld now. All the light didn't make it look any better than the rest of the neighborhood. It just made it easier to see how shabby everything was.

I parked three blocks away on Second Street, where the storefronts were mostly covered with yellowing newsprint or plywood. As I walked up Market, the stores began to look like they had some daytime trade, even if there were bars on most of the windows. One doorway was being used as a bedroom by a man wearing paint-spattered overalls and no shirt. He was laid out on a cardboard mat he'd made by cutting open a batch of fruit cartons, and he slept like a corpse at a wake.

The Blacklight was on the corner of Market and Fifth. To distinguish itself from its competitors, the front was completely dark. No neon. No lights. The windows had been painted over black. The only sign was an unlit naked light bulb over the door. This unassuming front, coupled with its location at the end of the block, helped make the Blacklight the favorite of S.A. queens who wanted to go slumming but be discreet about it.

Inside, the lighting wasn't much better. After passing through a second door, I found myself at one end of a fifteen-foot bar, which ran along the close wall all the way to the back. The bar top was painted red but had been scuffed to white in some places. A padded black leather armrest lined the side of the bar where the drinkers sat. On the bartender's side there was a door with a brightly lit square posing as a diamond that must have let into the kitchen. Next to an out-of-order phone, another door led to the toilets. They were still marked 'M' and 'F.' On the opposite wall was a row of booths with black leather cushions, some of which were intact, some of which had been repaired with tire patches, and some of which had bits of their yellow stuffing spilling out. A narrow row of two-top tables divided the bar from the booths. There were maybe a dozen patrons spread out across the room. I sat down at the closest stool.

The bartender came over with his arms crossed over his apron. They were big arms and tattooed, and they went with the rest of his physique. He looked like a boxer who no longer fought in the ring but stayed in shape because it was all he knew how to do. They come in all sizes, I guessed, but maybe he wasn't like that and just worked there. Maybe he had been here from before it turned into a queer joint. Maybe he couldn't stand his job but it was a job and who could argue with that? Right now his brow was pulled into an angry V. He hated somebody.

I put a five-dollar bill on the bar and ordered a gin and tonic. His look grew nastier, but he made the drink and set it on a paper napkin in front of me with a scowl. He didn't touch the five-dollar bill. He watched me sip my drink. Then he said, "We're paid up for the month."

"I'm not a cop," I said.

"You sure look like a cop. And we're all paid."

"I'm not a cop," I said again, and took another sip of my gin and tonic. Just a sip, because I didn't know how many drinks I was going to have to order in how many bars before I got something. "I'm looking for Greg Taylor. Does he come in here?"

"I wouldn't know," the man said, his arms crossed again. There was a nervous quiet among the other patrons, but I didn't look to see if they were watching.

"Would you know the names of any of your regulars?"

"No. I'm not too good with names."

I leaned in, pressing myself against the bar, ignoring the complaint from my bruised ribs. "Look, I'm not a cop, I'm a private detective. The man's family is worried about him. I'm just trying to find where he is and if he's okey."

"I don't know any Greg Taylor."

"I thought you weren't good with names. You remembered that one all right."

He didn't have an answer to that other than to shift his weight from one foot to the other.

"Look, I'm not trying to stir up any trouble. My client

doesn't want that either. Could you just give me a yes or a no if he comes in here? He's a pretty man, about my height, tan skin, light hair, small, feminine features, couldn't weigh more than one-thirty, probably less."

His face grew even emptier. "I don't know," he said pointedly, giving each word its own time in the spotlight.

I did look around at the other patrons then. Greg Taylor wasn't among them. No one appeared to be giving our conversation too much attention. Just a group of men enjoying their beer. To anyone who didn't know better it looked like a regular crowd of steady drinkers. I brought my eyes back to the bartender, but I said in a louder voice, "If you hear anything about Greg Taylor, you let me know."

I left the rest of my drink when I got up and put my card on the five-dollar bill. The money hadn't bought anything but you never knew when a five was going to be remembered at the right time. I glanced over the patrons again, but no one seemed to have reacted to my announcement. "Don't think too hard," I said.

"Don't come back," the bartender said.

"You must get a lot of repeat business talking that way," I said. He didn't care to respond. I went out through both of the doors and back into the glare of the street.

There was a group of three streetwalkers on the opposite corner now. I crossed and they saw me coming and started in with their propositions until they got a good look at me and turned away as though they were waiting for a bus. They all looked young, no more than twenty-five but probably younger. One of them was dressed in women's clothing, a long, slinky kimono wrap with matching slippers that weren't meant for wearing out of the house. His makeup made it almost hard to tell he wasn't a she, but only almost. The other two wore suit pants that were too tight on their already thin frames and untucked white shirts with the top three buttons left open and shoes that needed polishing. One had sunken cheeks and pallid skin with a slight sheen to it in the streetlight. I made him for a junky. None of them had hats.

"Can I buy anyone a drink?" I said. All three heads turned studiously away from me, doing what they could to catch the shadows from the next block. "I just have a few questions. The people on the block don't seem very friendly."

"We got nothing to say to you, copper," the he-she said, still with his head turned.

"I'm not a cop," I said. I was starting to wonder if I was, I had to say it so much. "I'm just looking for someone who I was told comes down here. For his folks."

The he-she turned then. "Peeper, huh?" he said. There was a reedy lilt to his voice and a softness around the edges, but it wasn't fooling anyone. "We've got nothing to say to peepers either. Unless you're looking for a good time."

I ignored that, took out my wallet and brought out another five. I held it where they could see it. "All I'm looking for is the whereabouts of a particular person. Easy money." I waited, but none of them made a move for the money. The two dressed in regular clothes shifted on their feet and looked up and down the block. They couldn't talk. Most of their customers had a wife and kids and a whole ordinary life in the city. The boys who worked in The Market were partially paid for confidentiality. I put the money away, and said, "Fine." I started to turn around, and one of them spoke.

"What's the name?" It was an unsteady voice. It came from the junky. His companions eyed him with upper lips curled in disgust.

I turned back and watched them as I said, "Greg Taylor." There was no flash of recognition. Just the same shiftiness. I was making them nervous. "Fine," I said again and went across the street and into the bar next to the Blacklight, a place called Jillian's. Stark had mentioned only the Blacklight and Choices by name, but that was because those were the bars that someone of his caliber might know about. I had a feeling that Taylor was just as likely to be known at any of the places along the block.

Jillian's was no different than the Blacklight. The tables were up front and the bar was in back and the lighting was better and there was a small platform in one corner with a drum kit, a standup base, and a trumpet beside a stool, but it was the same anyway. The same eyes looked at me. The same eyes made sure to look away. The bartender gave me the same business. I looked around, but nobody dared a second glance in my direction. As I watched, three Negroes came out from the back and went to the stage, resuming their positions at the instruments. The trumpet player counted a beat with his foot, and they all started together, a fast number that the patrons shouted over to be heard. The band didn't need the audience; they were making music. I left another five. No Greg Taylor. No anything. I didn't even touch my drink.

I went outside. It was getting later and there were more men on the street now. Different music could be heard coming from a few of the joints, clashing in the night. A faint breeze stirred the air, carrying the briny smell of the Pacific from only a block away, but it didn't make the night any cooler. As people passed me they hardly noticed I was there. They didn't like my look and I didn't like theirs. Only two of the whores were standing on their corner. I was probably wasting my time out there, but I didn't have a better idea, and the thought of going home to lick my wounds made me feel sorry for myself, and I didn't like feeling sorry for myself.

At the third bar, after going through the same routine with a blond-haired bartender wearing a too-tight shirt, my eyes caught on a face as I made my quick survey of the place. It was the junky from outside. He drew a few knowing glances from some of the men at the tables but he kept his eyes on the back of the bar, heading for the toilets. As I watched him, his eyes flicked at me and then away just for a moment. He went into the bathroom. I nursed my gin and tonic. The bartender had gone to the other end of the bar, finished with me. After ten minutes the junky still hadn't come out of the bathroom. I pushed off of the bar and went to the front door. If the junky wanted to find me, he would find me once he had worked up his nerve. For all I knew, he was just getting high.

The storefront next door was an all-night liquor store without any customers. I skipped that because Greg Taylor had not looked like the kind of man who ever bought his own liquor, and because when you go out at night to get back at your lover, you don't do it with a bottle bought at a liquor store.

The next bar was Choices. It was more of a dance hall than the other places. A five-piece band was playing fast numbers in a corner under a palm tree in a pot. The dance floor took up the center of the room, lit with spot-lights recessed into the ceiling that made white shiny spots on the wooden boards. There were several couples dancing and I wondered how they knew who should lead. The tables nearest the dance floor were filled, but the ones further out were empty. The bar was a classy thing with a gilt framed mirror along the back and lights under the glass shelves where the liquor was kept so that the various bottles shone and were reflected and shone some more. I didn't bother to try my line on the bartender over the sound of the band. Instead, I waited at the bar and watched the dancers. They could really dance.

After a minute or two, the junky streetwalker came in through the front door. He saw me looking at him and I smiled and he immediately looked away. A man at a nearby table called to him and he went over and let the man hold his hand, all the while looking at a spot on the table that was a thousand miles away. I watched them for a moment, the seated man pulling on the junky's arm, waving at the chair across the table from him, the junky just standing there with his head bowed and no expression on his face. I didn't want to watch anymore. There was no reason I had to. I turned my back and drank my drink all the way down. The liquor spread out in my body, reminding me that life was just life and it wasn't good or bad. I turned around again and the junky was now sitting at the table. He wouldn't stay long. I needed some fresh air. It was getting stuffy in there.

Outside, I smoked a cigarette, and when I'd finished with that one I lit another. Down at the end of the block, only the man dressed in pants and the unbuttoned shirt was standing under the streetlight. Maybe the getup with the kimono was good for business. I had started my third cigarette when the junky came out of the club. He stopped short when he saw me standing there. "You can follow me around all night and not get anywhere or we can just talk now," I said.

He looked down the block where his companion was standing watching him back.

"We can go somewhere else," I said.

"Meet me on Seaside at Sixth," he said without looking at me.

"You've got something to tell me?"

He didn't answer, already walking back down towards his street corner.

I turned in the other direction, making it quick to get to the end of the block and turned right on Sixth towards the ocean.

TWENTY

He came up on Seaside walking along the closed-up shops, well out of the glow of the streetlamps. He kept his head down, shooting occasional glances behind him as though he were afraid of being followed. When he was three feet away, he stopped, glanced up at me once, and then back down at the sidewalk. He was even younger than I had first thought, probably no more than eighteen. He looked sickly and every half a minute he would shiver as though it wasn't seventy-five degrees out. He was a real nervous one. I wondered how he got any business.

"You have something to tell me?" I said, trying to make him look me in the eye.

"Where's the money?"

I got out my wallet and took out the five-dollar bill I had shown them on the street corner, or one exactly like it. "This isn't for nothing," I said, not yet holding out the bill. "You've got to have something to tell me."

"I've got something. Now give me the money."

"What's your name?"

His expression turned suspicious. "Why?"

"So I have something to call you by. Just a name. Your street name."

"Rusty," he said, the name foreign on his tongue.

"Okey, Rusty." I held the bill out to him and he snatched it away faster than I thought he could move. It disappeared.

"How long did it take you to learn to get the money first?" I said.

He looked up at me with his eyes without moving his head. He didn't like me very much. Even if I had given him the money. His eyes went back to the street. "I know Greg from a while back," he said.

I waited for him to say more. When he didn't, I said, "And?"

"We had the same dealer. A guy named Renaldo who works on the boardwalk. I can take you to him."

"When was the last time you saw him? Taylor, I mean."

He shrugged and tilted his head. "Six months. Maybe eight."

"But you can take me to the guy he used to get his junk from maybe eight months ago?"

He bobbed his head emphatically. "Yeah."

"That doesn't sound like five dollars to me."

The eyes flicked again. "Look, man. If anyone's gonna know anything about Greg, it's going to be Renaldo. Anyone who's gonna tell you anything anyway."

Junkies will scam you any way they can to get a buck. But I didn't have a better lead. "Well. Let's go meet Renaldo."

He bobbed his head again, rocking on his feet as well, and then stepped off the sidewalk into the street. It was only after he stepped off that he looked both ways. Seaside was deserted at that time of night anyway. You would never know that just around the corner was a burgeoning nightlife.

We stayed on Sixth, going the half a block that ended at the boardwalk in a sandy cul-de-sac. A wooden lattice blocked off the black space under the boardwalk. There were stairs on either side of the street, each step with a bar of sand on its back edge. I could hear the ocean now and the salty smell was stronger. We took the stairs on the south side of the street and as soon as we stepped out onto the boards, we were met by a cool, steady wind. There were no lights on the boardwalk or stores or concessions here. It was just a raised set of boards with a railing on either side and steps down to the beach. At regular intervals were wooden park benches. There were silhouetted figures on most of the benches, standing out against the darkness that was the ocean and the sky.

Rusty turned north and I followed alongside him. Neither of us spoke. He seemed less nervous, less jumpy, but it could just have been that it wasn't as obvious when he was walking. The wind blew my tie, making it flutter up against me and over my shoulder. My coat rippled and I had to put my hand on my hat a couple of times. As we walked, the sounds of couples on the benches came as a soft murmur, and then there were the occasional loud voices lost in the darkness of the beach. In the distance, the nighttime lights of Harbor City's commercial boardwalk shone like a mirage for the night traveler, the rides stretching away from the land almost all the way down to the water, a flashing neon peninsula. There was a lot of darkness between The Market and the lights of the tourists' playland.

We had gone maybe five blocks when Rusty made a move for a street-side stairwell. We were still at least ten blocks away from the carnival lights, a good walk, but not an impossible one. This location would allow Renaldo to service customers from either community. We clopped down the stairs, grains of sand crunching under our heels. In the darkness of the corner made by the staircase and the wooden lattice stood a man in a sharp blue suit with a purple shirt and a purple tie. He wasn't Mexican, as his name had suggested, but rather a pale and doughy-faced man with deep-set eyes and a cocky smirk that looked like a permanent fixture. The clothes were expensive and unnecessarily flamboyant, an affectation like the name, but maybe good for business, like the whore's kimono.

"Hey, Renaldo," Rusty said as we came up to him.

Renaldo's eyes ignored Rusty and held my own. "Can I help you?" he said. His voice left no doubt that he was in charge or at least thought he was. He probably had a piece tucked under his arm. That made him invincible.

"Yeah, five dollars," Rusty said, the bill magically reappearing in his hand. His voice was wrought with eagerness.

"Can I help you?" Renaldo said again, his eyes still on mine.

"Oh, yeah," Rusty said, half turning towards me. "This guy's a dick. He's looking for Greg."

"Why would you come to me?"

"Yeah, I don't know," Rusty said. "But I've got five dollars. That's enough for plenty."

I decided it was time I spoke for myself. "I was hired by Greg Taylor's family to make sure he's all right. He doesn't even have to go home. I just need to talk to him."

"Again, why would you come to me?"

"Once a junky always a junky," I said.

He laughed, one short bark. He liked that. It was amusing to him. He liked me now. "All right, peeper. That's rich."

"I don't care what you're doing here. I just need a line on Mr. Taylor."

"You've got nothing?" His eyes were lights in the shadows.

I held out my hands to show just how empty they were.

He thought about it. Then he gave a half-shrug. "Greg came by last night, as a matter of fact. He was with some guy. Tall, good-looking guy. I don't know him."

"Did you hear a name?"

"John, or Tim, or Tom. Something simple like that."

I nodded to show I was listening. "What time was this?"

"Late. Maybe three in the A.M. They bought some stuff, and went up on the boards."

"Did they say where they were going?"

"Didn't have to say. I could hear them under the board-walk. Must have gone there to get high and get cozy. Certainly sounded like it."

"Sounded like what?"

He just smiled. "Sounded like *it*, shamus." He unleashed his bark again. Rusty was almost hopping from one foot to the other now. "That's all I know."

"They didn't come back out?"

"Not that I saw, but that doesn't mean anything. They could have come off of the boardwalk at any of these streets."

I nodded.

"Who'd you say you were working for? Greg doesn't have any family."

"My client would prefer to stay anonymous."

That warranted a bark as well. I was a funny man. I was really cracking him up. "I like you, dick."

"Renaldo," Rusty said. "Come on."

Renaldo continued to ignore him. "I hope you know this isn't all free," Renaldo said.

"It's not much. You're going to get my five in a moment."

"That's his five. And five doesn't sound like a lot right now."

"What makes you think it's worth more?"

"You had nothing and now you have something. You gave this junky five bucks just to bring you to me."

The man had a point. And anyway John Stark was footing the bill. I brought out my wallet and dug out a ten. He took it from me and then turned to Rusty to conduct his business. I was dismissed. I wasn't anywhere. I had nowhere to go. I had let an innocent woman get turned into a murder suspect and now I was letting my one remaining client down. I wouldn't hire me. I took the stairs back up to the boardwalk and then the ones across the way down to the beach. I don't know why. It was something to do.

TWENTY-ONE

From the beach, the carnival lights took on a sad, hope-less appearance. They were insignificant when compared with the dark surging body of water churning and crashing and whispering some forty yards away. There was just enough light to make out the water's movement but little else. The spot at which the ocean ended and the sky began was lost to the darkness.

My shoes slid on the sand and sank, and I could feel wet grains pour in around the sides of my feet. I hobbled awkwardly around the stairs with the grit weighing me down. The wind from the shore chilled me.

On the beach side, there was no wooden lattice blocking entry to the black space under the boardwalk. I got my penlight out and used it to paint the space between two support beams right in front of me. It allowed me to see only about six inches ahead. But the ground was more even there, and there was enough room to stand up without crouching. I walked forward slowly, my light pointed down with an occasional sweep upwards to be sure I wasn't about to knock my head against a support. I didn't know what I expected to find. The sand was lit-tered with empty cans, crumpled newsprint, and candy bar wrappers, along with shells, rocks, and some scrub brush. There were also empty paper envelopes, discarded needles, and plenty of cigarette butts, showing that the

spot under the boardwalk where Renaldo sold was a pop-
ular place for those of his customers who couldn't wait to
get indoors for their fix.

I walked straight back until I was at the lattice that
separated me from the street. Renaldo was standing on
the other side, leaning against the stairwell, smoking a
cigarette. The syrupy flavor of the smoke told me it
wasn't tobacco he was smoking. I played my flash on the
ground in either direction, but there was nothing to see. I
was searching just to be doing something, to convince
myself that I wasn't entirely useless. I'd do better at
home in bed. My head hadn't touched a pillow in nearly
forty-eight hours. My little nap courtesy of Mitch hardly
counted.

I picked my way back towards the beach. The debris
crackled under my feet and my shoes now felt as though
they weighed an extra two pounds each. I had veered off
to the right in the dark, and was coming out under the
stairs. I started to correct my path when the edge of my
penlight beam caught the scuffed sole of a man's shoe.
That didn't surprise me. It was just one more thing that
might get discarded under the boardwalk. But then I
traced my flash up a little more and saw that the shoe was
still attached to a leg. It was attached to a leg wearing
familiar pale blue suit pants. I crouched as the stairs
came down above me and my penlight lit up the pile that
was wedged under them. A man could have decided it
was an out of the way place to spend the night. He probably wouldn't sleep face down though.

I knew who it was but I had to make sure. I lifted his
head by the hair enough to see his face. It was a pretty

face, a strange, half-grown, boyish face. Mr. Greg Taylor was never going to fight with Stark again. He was never going to fight with anybody.

I let his head drop, hiding the face back in the sand, and I felt my way along his body, training the flash on my hand. There was nothing in his pants pockets and he didn't have any others. He could have been robbed, but it was just as likely that he had had nothing in his pockets in the first place. His was a nameless body and would have remained such if found by someone who didn't know him. That would have set the police back days and whoever did it would have plenty of time to distance himself from the crime. Assuming there was a crime, and he hadn't died of a self-inflicted overdose. Even then, his companion, John or Tim or Tom, would want to have been somewhere else when it happened. Especially if "John" was John Stark and this whole case was a preemptive ruse.

I came out from under the boardwalk and stretched in the open air. I made my way back up the stairs, pushing away the idea of what was underneath, and then crossed the deserted boardwalk and came down the other set of stairs to the street. At the bottom, I leaned against the railing and emptied first one shoe and then the other, adding my share to a little mound of sand where other people had done the same. I walked back around to Renaldo. Rusty was long gone.

"You have anything else to add to the noises you heard last night?"

"Just noises, peeper," Renaldo said and let out a laugh filled with smoke.

I looked back along the street to Seaside and the block beyond. This was a commercial district. It probably closed up at six o'clock just when the boardwalk was starting to draw business away for the night. "There a phone nearby?" I said.

"At the end of the block. Who do you need to call?"

I looked at him. "Let's just say you might not want to hang around here to find out."

He straightened up. "Why do you want to do that?"

"Take a peek under those stairs on the other side of the boardwalk and you'll see."

He spat a word that conveyed the full range of his feelings.

"I'll leave you out of it by name," I said, "but I can't promise to leave you out completely. I guess the police will still know who I mean."

He spat the word again, and then said, "I hate junkies," only he included the adjectival version of his new favorite word there too.

"Don't worry too much. The police won't be too happy to see me again either."

He nodded ruefully. "You too, huh? You too."

We turned to go then, and walked the half-block together without speaking. At the corner, Renaldo pointed out the phone in silence, and then turned north on Seaside and walked briskly away.

The phone booth was wood without a door. The inside surface had been carved with any number of names, initials, suggestions, and complaints. I picked up the receiver and dialed a number. I ran my hand over the booth's wall, feeling the scrape of the cut words.

A voice came on the line. I was surprised that it didn't sound sleepy. In this deserted part of town it felt like the dead of night.

"Mr. Stark, please," I said.

"Mr. Stark is no longer receiving calls this evening," the voice said. It was the butler who had opened the door that morning, a lifetime ago.

"Tell him it's Dennis Foster about Greg Taylor," I said.

There was a moment's hesitation, and then the voice said, "Please hold the wire."

I held the wire.

"You found him," Stark's famous voice said after several minutes. There was the sound of another extension being hung up. "I knew you were good. I have a sense for these things."

"You may not think so when you hear the rest of it."

A note of caution entered the baritone. "Go on."

"He's dead."

A sharp intake of breath sounded over the line. There was a moment in which he collected himself, preparing before going on. When he spoke, his voice had lost its usual tone of command, but there was nothing else to indicate that he was upset. "What happened?"

I told him. I left out that Greg had been seen with another man.

There was a pause. At last, "Did he suffer?"

"I'm not a doctor, but it didn't look like it."

"Good," he said.

"I need to call it in, and I want to know what you'd like me to say. I'm down in Harbor City and the police are going to want to know why."

"I don't know," he said.

"Where were you last night?"

"Home. Why?"

"Anybody with you? Was anyone else in the house last night?"

"My butler was in. I asked him for some coffee at, I don't know, ten o'clock, maybe later. The maids were in also. They'd all vouch for me. But why does that matter? Wasn't it the drugs? We'd fought about that so many times; Greg always promised to quit." His voice had grown tight and risen half an octave. "Damn him. It was an overdose, wasn't it?"

"I don't know."

"So you think I'm a suspect?"

"No, but the police are going to. Did Greg know Mandy Ehrhardt?"

"They might have met once or twice. Why? Does this have anything to do with that?"

"No. I can't see how it does. I'm just thinking of ways to leave you out and I don't see any."

"That's all right. You do what you have to. The police have always been kind to me before."

"These aren't S.A. cops. They're Harbor City cops. They don't tend to be kind to anybody. You told me Greg was on your payroll. Was he really or was that just a story?"

"He is. He was. He always claimed he didn't like it, that it made him feel like a kept man. I always thought it was a good precaution."

"It was. People will guess the truth, there's no avoiding

that, but it should mean that everyone keeps to the story officially at least. I can't speak for Parsons and Hopper."

"I can't worry about that," he said. He paused. "Thank you. For finding him."

"I'll call tomorrow if I know any more. The police may be there tonight. This phone call never happened. They don't like me very much already. I don't need to give them another excuse. Your butler…?"

"Nothing to worry about," he said without any hesitation.

"I'll call tomorrow," I said, and hung up. I picked up the phone again and called the police.

TWENTY-TWO

It was only five minutes before a prowl car pulled up alongside me. In this neighborhood at night they probably had a black-and-white every ten blocks, so I wasn't too impressed with the timing. They popped the spotlight on. I hadn't finished my first cigarette yet, so I let them watch me smoke it. The passenger door opened and a uniformed officer stepped out. "You call the cops?" he shouted from behind the safety of his open door.

"Yeah. That was me," I said.

He looked in the open car and said something and then he shouted over at me again, "Where's this body?"

"Under the boardwalk," I said, and started down the block without waiting for them.

The door slammed behind me and there were rapid footsteps and the sound of an engine being gunned. The car lurched ahead of me, pulling to a stop at the end of the block where Renaldo had been standing ten minutes before. I hoped the smell of his marijuana hadn't lingered. The cop who had called to me came up behind and said, "Stop right there."

I stopped. His partner got out of the patrol car and went over to the wooden lattice at the end of the street. The spot from the car was still on, and he peered through the holes trying to make out Greg Taylor's body. I finished my cigarette and threw away the butt.

"There's a body all right," the partner called.

"Turn around, buddy, and give it to me slow."

I turned around and said, "If you don't mind, I'll wait for the homicide boys. I hate to repeat myself."

The cop was young, at the utmost twenty, and the attempt at swagger in his posture was laughable. He wore his hair in a military crew, which made his hat fit him loosely. He had his hand on the butt of his gun and looked a little too eager to draw.

His partner came up. He was older, thicker in the gut but more comfortable in his own skin. He wore wire-rimmed glasses with round lenses. "How'd you find him?"

"He don't want to talk," the younger one said. "Wants to wait for the homicide boys."

"I just don't want to waste any of our time," I said. "You know in five minutes you won't have anything more to do with this."

The cop in glasses shrugged and started to walk back towards Seaside Avenue. His partner stepped to the side so that he was within his partner's path but still had his eye on me. "Carter, we need to watch this guy. What's he doing out here at this time of night?"

Carter didn't stop. "He's a dick, wetbrain. He's out here because he's snooping."

The younger cop trained his eye back on me, and I gave him a smile and reached for another cigarette. His hands jumped to his gun again until he saw the cigarette and matches in my hand. "You're a dick?" he said to me, jutting his chin to show he was in control.

"You want to see my license?" I said.

"Yeah," he said. So I got out my license and held it out to him. He stepped close enough to read it and then stepped back. "What are you doing out here?"

I didn't say anything. An unmarked car pulled up alongside Carter, who took a step back on the sidewalk. A short man in plain clothes got out the passenger side and started in our direction without waiting for his partner. He wore a brown felt hat with a yellow feather in the brim. His face was a closed fist. He had a pocket notebook out and was writing in it with a pencil as he approached. Carter fell in beside him. His partner brought up the rear. He was broad at the shoulders and not much narrower below. His blue shirt required quite a lot of yardage and even so there wasn't enough at the collar for him to close the button comfortably. His knotted necktie rode halfway down his chest. The three of them walked past without a glance at me or my young interrogator. They went up the stairs to the boardwalk and then were out of sight. A moment later a flash could be seen under the stairs.

I smoked my cigarette. The young cop watched me smoke it.

Eventually the other three came back. Carter went to his patrol car and got in it. The small man and his broad-shouldered partner came up to me. As they approached, the short one said, "Where's Renaldo? Make sure they bring him in." The big man nodded. Then the small man addressed me, "I'm Captain Langstaff, this is Detective Graham. You are?"

"He's a private dick from S.A., Captain."

The captain looked over at the kid, and then back at his notebook. "Graham, show Officer Stephens how to get into his cruiser. Maybe he and Carter can find Renaldo."

Graham stepped around and the kid actually took a step back as though he expected to be punched. He then walked in a wide arc around all of us and went back to the cruiser. He opened the passenger door still looking back at us as though we were planning to attack him. He called, "We'll find Renaldo," and then he climbed into the car.

Graham walked back, stopping when he was just behind my shoulder, visible out of the corner of my eye.

The captain left his eyes on his notebook. "Private dick from S.A."

"That's right. Dennis Foster. Do you want my story?"

"Hmm-mm," Langstaff said.

"I'm working a missing persons job. A fairy, so I went to The Market to ask around. Nobody knew anything, naturally."

"Naturally."

"But then a junky said he knew where my man scored his dope. He brought me here."

He nodded, writing in his notebook the whole time. "You talk to Renaldo?"

"I didn't ask him his name."

"Doesn't matter." Langstaff looked up. "And the body, is he your man?"

I nodded. "Greg Taylor."

"Who are you working for?"

"I'd rather not say."

The folds in his forehead deepened.

"But I won't insult your intelligence. It'll take you ten minutes to find out. John Stark."

"The movie actor?"

I nodded again.

Langstaff said something under his breath. I couldn't make out the words, but I got the idea. He nodded to Graham. "Check his license. Get his info." He looked at me. "Is there anything you're not telling me?"

"Nothing that I think is relevant."

"It's not your place to make that decision, Mr. Foster, but honestly, some fairy o.d.ing that's going to be covered up anyway, I don't really give a damn." He walked back towards the beach again, and started up the stairs.

"You're his new favorite person," Graham said behind me. "Let's see the paperwork."

I got out my wallet again and handed the whole thing to him. He took out his own notebook and wrote down all the details in careful tight letters.

I threw away my butt and waited for Graham to finish. The night was cooling off, especially near the water. My chest hurt when I breathed, and the exhaustion of the last two days had finally hit me. My knees were suddenly unsure if they wanted to keep working in my employ.

Graham tapped the wallet on my shoulder and I reached up and took it. "Got a car?" he said. He was a gentle giant. He was a pal. Don't believe what they say about cops. They're there to protect and to serve.

"On Second."

"Okey, get going. We'll call if we need you."

The meat wagon pulled up then, taking the spot where the black-and-white had been parked. A wizened-looking man with a large black leather case got out and started for the boardwalk stairs.

I bowed my head and left.

TWENTY-THREE

It was almost two in the morning when I stepped out of the automatic elevator onto my floor in the Olmstead. The injuries from Mitch's thoughtful beating had settled into one continuous ache that covered my body from my neck to my hips. I pulled out my keys, and separated the apartment door key from the others on the ring. Halfway down the hall a phone was ringing. Its shrill insistent call was the only sound on the floor, a nasty, unwelcome sound at this time of night that could only mean bad news, somebody died, you're wanted at the hospital. When I got closer, I could hear that it was my phone. It was the same noise I had walked away from nearly five hours ago; as though it had been ringing the entire time I was gone.

I got the door opened and crossed to the phone without turning on the lights. "Foster."

"I've been trying to get in touch with you all night." The accent was thicker in his panic.

"Well you have me now, Miguel. What is it?"

"Miss Rose, she's not well."

"Was she ever?"

"No, you don't understand, she wants to die. She cut her wrists."

I let out my breath like I'd been thumped on the chest, and I didn't have to imagine what that felt like either. "When did this happen?"

"I tried calling you many hours ago. At dinner time at least."

"Why didn't you call the police?"

"She wouldn't have wanted..." He trailed off.

No, she probably wouldn't. They couldn't have helped much anyway, and they might have taken the act as an admission of guilt. But surely someone could have helped. Anyone could have more than me. "How is she now?" I asked.

"She's sleeping. I gave her some pills. I've been keeping her pills away from her for many months now. The doctor didn't think it was safe for her to have them. But I didn't know what else to do..." He was getting worked up again.

My mind was racing. Something wasn't making sense. "Keep an eye on her. I'll be right there."

"Thank you. I'll leave the door unlocked so you don't have to ring."

I hadn't had to ring once yet, but I didn't bother pointing that out. I hung up and went back out into the hall.

The streets were mostly empty at that time of night. The city's neon still flashed and blinked, reflected in chrome façades and plate glass store windows, even as the stores themselves were dark. In the residential district, all of the house lights were out, giving the impression of an abandoned city whose traffic lights flashed red and green for no one. I made the turn onto Highlawn Drive and parked in the driveway this time. Unlike the neighbors, the Rosenkrantz house was lit up with what appeared to be every light they had.

Once more Miguel opened the door for me before I

could reach for the knob. "She's sleeping still, upstairs in her room."

"Where's Mr. Rosenkrantz?"

Miguel shook his head. "I don't know. He hasn't been home since morning. At dinnertime, Miss Rose started to get very excited. I tried to call you. Where were you?"

"Out. Give me the rest."

"She started shouting. Then she locked herself in her room. After a time, she quieted down, and at first I thought this was good, but when I stopped hearing any sounds at all...I went in with another key."

"Did she know you had another key?"

"Yes."

"Then what?"

"She was on the floor in the bathroom with her wrists cut. There was blood, but not so much. I bandaged her arms and carried her to her bed, gave her the pills, and I've been calling you ever since."

"When was the last time you checked on her?"

"Every ten minutes."

It sounded believable. It also sounded like a head-strong movie star who needed drama in her life as well as in her pictures. Knox had mentioned that she was prone to moods, and I had seen that. But no one had said any-thing about suicide.

"Take me up," I said.

We went up the staircase opposite the one that led to Rosenkrantz's study, along the catwalk hallway, past two closed doors to a third that had been left ajar. Miguel knocked enough to satisfy propriety and then opened the door the rest of the way.

The only source of light here was a pair of wall sconces made to look like lit candles in brass candelabras. There was one to either side of the four-poster bed. The soft glare from each shone on the green patterned wallpaper, turning the wall at those spots yellow. There was a nice chandelier in the center of the ceiling that wasn't doing anything but looking pretty. An open door just past the bed was the bathroom.

She was on the side of the bed nearest us, propped up on throw pillows of varying sizes, all with gilt tassels and somber colors except for the pillow just below her head, a normal pillow in a normal white pillowcase, good for sleeping no matter your station. The bedclothes had been pulled back on that side of the bed to form a nice triangle of exposed sheet. She hadn't pulled the covers back over herself. Her right hand lay on the white cloth. A handkerchief had been wrapped around her wrist, and I had no doubt there was one on the other wrist as well. The whole scene looked like a sick room out of a movie, and I wondered if wherever Chloë Rose was it always looked like a movie.

Miguel went to her side. "Miss Rose, Miss Rose, it's Mr. Foster. He's here to help." She didn't stir. He looked back at me with open honest eyes filled with worry. It was plain that he was in love with her. It was a bad thing for him to be.

I stepped past him and took her right hand. I turned it over and unwound the white handkerchief from her wrist. Either she hadn't been very serious about dying or she didn't know what she was doing. There were two jagged cuts across her wrist, not up it, and they intersected as though she had been unsure of the first one and tried again. They were more than superficial, but they wouldn't need stitches. The blood had already clotted, and there was hardly more than a small rusty stain on the handker-chief. I reached across her for the other one just to make sure. It was the same.

As I replaced her left hand, her eyes flickered, and she said something in French in the dull dreamy voice of the drugged. She said a little bit more, and then opened her eyes again, this time enough to maybe see me. She switched to English then. "I'm not dead."

"Did you hope to be?" I said.

She closed her eyes and licked her lips. "Could I please have some water?"

Miguel went around the bed to the bathroom. There was the sound of the sink going on and then off, and he brought the glass to her. He had to put it in her hand, and once he did she just held it, resting the glass on the bed, making no effort to actually drink.

"If you want to kill yourself by slitting your wrists," I said, "you need to cut along the veins up your forearm. That's how you'll bleed out. Slashing across your wrists will just hurt more than anything else."

"I wondered," she said, "why there was so little blood."

"Why do you want to kill yourself? Because you've got an alcoholic husband and some policemen weren't very nice to you?"

Miguel shifted behind me, and I knew that he wasn't happy with the way I was talking to her. Well, he had called me, so I was what he was going to get.

She shook her head back and forth on the pillow, slowly.

"You want to go to a hospital?" I said. "You think that'll get you away from all of this?"

"I don't want a hospital," she said, a petulant child. "I don't want anything. I don't want to be alive."

"You can quit playing Madame Bovary," I told her. "Nobody really thinks you have anything to do with this murder. The police just want to catch a few headlines."

"It's not about the police." Her voice was stronger now. It sounded more like a cornered animal than an injured one.

"Maybe at Merton Stein they like it when you pull your prima donna act, it makes them feel like they've got a real star, but out here, it's not getting you anything."

"You think this is an act?"

"Mister Foster," Miguel said behind me.

"Yeah. I think you're feeling upstaged by a dead starlet who was having an affair with your husband. You've got to remind everyone you're around, but all you got was a Mexican and me."

"Mister Foster," Miguel said again, putting his hand on my elbow now.

"No," Chloë Rose said, throwing the water glass. She only had enough strength to get it a foot or so away from the bed. The water splashed my pant leg. She was shaking her head. "No. No, no, no. I have no one anymore. My mother…my father…Now my husband, too. I have nobody! Nobody wants me."

Miguel left then. Probably going back to his stash of medicine.

"What about your adoring fans? Hell, I'm waiting for your next picture."

She just kept shaking her head.

Miguel was back then with another glass of water and some pills cupped in his palm. I held up my hand to prevent him from going forward. "She's had enough of that."

She pushed what covers were on her off and stood, but she was unsteady on her feet and she fell against me. "Hold me," she said. I put my arms around her. It hurt like hell.

Our faces were inches apart. Her eyes were desperate, urgent with need. Did she want me to kiss her? With her husband missing and her doting houseboy watching?

I held her away from me, one hand on each of her arms. "I know a private place," I said. "The Enoch White Clinic. I had some dealings with them a year or so back when I was working a missing persons and the missing person turned up...unwell. They're good, professional, real doctors."

"You think I need to go to hospital?"

"You think you're fine here?"

She rested her head against my chest. "I'm not fine anywhere."

"I'll ring them right up. They've got people on call any time of the day or night. I bet they can be here within the hour."

She looked back up at me, and now she was scared.

"It'll be all right," I said, although I didn't know if it would.

"But what happened to Mandy..."

"The police are looking into it. Sometimes they surprise you and do their job."

"You said the police only want headlines, not killers."

Throwing my own words back at me. I was as crazy as

she was to go on talking to her. But up close like that she smelled so nice. A man could get distracted by that.

She straightened a fold in my shirt, studying the weave intensely. "If you would look into it, I would feel so much better. Everyone else seems out for themselves. I'm frightened."

"I've been warned away from this thing by more people in more ways than I would care to list."

She looked up at me without moving her head. Her eyes glistened, just like they did at that crucial moment in all of her pictures. "Please," she said, breathing the word so I could feel it on my lips.

I bent down and mashed my lips against hers. It wasn't right, but I did it anyway, and I won't say I'm sorry. When we broke apart, I said, "Why does Daniel Merton want to buy your horse?"

Her brow crumpled, and she took a step back, both hands still on my chest. "What does that have to do with anything?"

"I don't know. That's why I'm asking you."

She shook her head, confused, and I could see the hysteria setting back in.

Miguel said, "Mr. Foster, I think you should leave."

We ignored that.

"When did he give you the horse," I said.

She still shook her head. "Four months ago, maybe five."

"Does he often give you things like that?"

"On occasion. When a picture does well. He does it with all of his actresses. It doesn't mean anything."

"Has he ever asked for a present he's given you back before?"

She pressed her lips together, and shook her head. Maybe this time it meant no. "I don't understand, why are you asking me these things?"

"Miss Rose," Miguel said.

"Forget it," I said, and then I leaned in, and she met me, and I kissed her again, smelling flowers and something behind the flowers that was really her.

This time when we parted, she said, "Promise me you'll help Mandy."

"I'll try," I said, because I was a fool.

She collapsed in my arms, going limp, and I struggled to hold her. I leaned her back so that she sat down on the bed, and then I turned back to Miguel, indicating that he should step in and take over. He wouldn't look at me. He took her arm and leaned down for her legs, helping her back onto the bed. There was a phone on the night table and I picked it up to call the clinic. They did the bulk of their business giving people the cure, booze and dope, but they handled all variety of mental disorders. I couldn't tell if Chloë Rose had a problem beyond an artistic bent, but if she was suicidal, she needed more than a Mexican with a pill bottle and a stack of handkerchiefs to sop up her blood. The nurse on the phone assured me that they'd be right over.

Miguel had gotten her back in the bed, and was holding a new glass of water to her lips. I didn't see if he had given her the pills too. I went back out into the hall, feeling that I had done what I could and a lot that I shouldn't have, and wondering how I had put myself back into this thing right when I should have been walking out. Miguel joined me in a moment.

"Don't be sore at me," I said. "I didn't mean for any of it to go that way in there."

"We're all doing our jobs," he said.

I was too exhausted to fight with him.

"These doctors that you called? Will they call the police?"

"No. And they'll do all they can to keep the police from her—to keep everyone from her, really."

He nodded as though that was satisfactory. We went back downstairs and smoked cigarettes in silence while we waited. When the men in white came, they were quick, cool, and professional. We watched Chloë Rose, the great star, led into the back of the white van that read "Enoch White Clinic" in red with a caduceus along the side. They pulled away with her.

"Tell Rosenkrantz where she went, if he ever comes back," I said. "He can call me if he wants to."

Miguel didn't say anything. I didn't care. I set a brisk pace to my car, got in, made it to my apartment building, and fell on the mattress without taking off my shoes.

TWENTY-FOUR

I missed the sunrise and missed most of what people call morning. I had to get undressed before I could get dressed again, which only hurt a little. No more than getting gored by a bull. I decided that I needed a proper breakfast. I brought out most of what was in the refrigerator and fried it in butter while the coffee brewed and then ate the whole mess in a little less time than it took to cook it. It was eleven o'clock. I had the vague sense that at some point the previous night, I had promised Chloë Rose that I would find Mandy Ehrhardt's killer. I distinctly remembered getting thrown off that very case by no less than three people, some more emphatic than others. And I didn't know if Greg Taylor's death tied in to all of this, but with Chloë Rose and Stark in the same picture, it felt a little too close for comfort. When you added that all up, I guessed there wasn't much to do except to go see if any more paint had peeled off of the walls in my office.

The waiting room at my office appeared empty when I opened the door. The standing ashtray had the usual number of butts plus the one that Knox had added the day before. The layer of dust on the rough burgundy upholstery was undisturbed. It was the appearance of no business, which was business as usual. I closed the outer door and turned to face the space behind it.

"That's far enough," Benny Sturgeon said, holding a .32 automatic in his right hand. The barrel pointed at me.

"When you want to hide in doorways, Mr. Sturgeon, it's best to leave off the aftershave," I said, like I was an expert at hiding in doorways.

He took a quick step towards me, but when I didn't move, he stepped back again. "I'm the one who's going to do the talking, you get me?"

I laughed, and the hard expression on his face turned to pained confusion.

"I've got a gun here," he said.

"You've been watching too many of your own movies."

I turned away from him to go to my office door.

"That's far enough," he said.

"You said that already," I reminded him while getting the key out and fitting it into the door. "When you want to threaten somebody, it's best to have the safety catch off. It makes the whole thing more effective."

He moved behind me, but I ignored him. Hollywood. The talent was crazy and the people behind the scenes were crazier. I opened the office door, and flicked on the overhead light.

There was a man standing against the opposite wall with his arms over his chest. He looked familiar, but I couldn't place him.

"Who the hell are you?" I said.

"My partner," a voice said behind me. "McEvoy. You met yesterday."

"How do you do," McEvoy said, bobbing his head.

"Samuels," I said, and turned to see him. "You couldn't

wait out front like a civilian would? You've got to break into my office?"

"It's not breaking in when there's probable cause," Detective Samuels said. "You're suspected of interfering with a police investigation." He looked over at Sturgeon, who had come in, his gun still outstretched. "You can drop that, Sturgeon," Samuels said.

"Don't mind him," I said. "It's just a prop. You've got blanks in there, don't you, Sturgeon?"

His hand dropped to his side and he was the same ineffectual man who had tried to hire me the day before. "Yes. They're blanks."

"And the safety's on," Samuels said.

"Okey, the damn safety's on!" Sturgeon said.

I nodded my chin at Samuels. "You mind if I sit down? I've kind of been running around the past few days." I went around my desk, pulled out the chair, and sat down like I was all alone, bringing my hands up behind my head and resting it on both of my palms. Samuels was still staring at the director. "What are you doing here?"

Sturgeon looked around at each of us like he was going to ask for directions.

"He came by yesterday," I said. "He wanted to hire me to work the Ehrhardt murder. He had this crazy idea that you wanted Chloë Rose for the spot. I told him I'd already been warned off of that case and anyway I've got a job going and I only work one job at a time. So he came back to change my mind."

"You know, I never saw his lips move," Samuels said, eliciting a choked-off laugh from his partner.

"Is that what it was all about?" Samuels said to Sturgeon.

"You thought you could scare the peeper into working this case?"

Sturgeon nodded. "Yes. It's all exactly as Mr. Foster says."

"What, you don't trust the cops?" McEvoy said.

"Do you?" I said.

"Okay, enough from you," Samuels said. "You know, Foster, the other morning I liked you all right, and I'm not a man who likes peepers."

"You're not alone."

He ignored that. "You played it straight with me. You didn't hold anything out." He looked at me sharply. "Did you?"

"No," I said, leaning forward in my chair and resting my hands on my desk.

"You see? He didn't leave anything out," Samuels said across the room to McEvoy as if they had been arguing about it before I got there. Samuels looked back at me. "So how come I find out you're working the Ehrhardt murder when I told you not to?"

"Who says I am?" I said, squinting.

"I say it," Samuels said. "And an informant who I won't mention. You'll understand."

"Did you find everything you needed in here, or do you need me to get out any other files for you?"

"This one's a real riot," McEvoy said.

"Who asked you?" I said.

"Enough. Just tell me what you found out, Foster, and then that's the end of it for you. Understand?

I nodded over at Sturgeon. "Do we want company while we talk?"

"Sturgeon, you wait outside," Samuels said.

Sturgeon slumped his shoulders, and went back out into the reception room. Samuels closed the door behind him. I listened for the sound of the outer door, but it didn't come. Sturgeon was waiting.

"So my friend at the *Chronicle* ratted me out," I said, taking a cigarette from the pack on my desk.

"Why do you say that?" Samuels said.

I waved out my match. "Only person who could have talked."

"You think what you want," Samuels said. "Just spill."

"I'm guessing you already know everything I know. There was a woman killed the same way as Ehrhardt back in December, just before Christmas. Found in Harbor City, never identified. So naturally I got to thinking that maybe they were killed by the same person. You see why I might have thought that?"

Samuels pressed his lips together and squinted. He saw all right. But it looked like it might have been the first time he saw. Maybe it hadn't been Fisher who had ratted me out after all.

"So who was the Jane Doe?" Samuels said.

"Never identified," I repeated, slower than before. "You can find everything I know in the *S.A. Times* for December 23."

"Fine," Samuels said. "What about this man under the boardwalk in Harbor City last night? Or did you think I hadn't heard about that?"

"A different job."

"He's connected to another actor in Ehrhardt's movie. I don't like that."

"You saying there's a connection between their deaths?"

"Am I?"

"Don't let me be the one to tell you," I said.

Samuels took a deep breath then and let it out. His whole face went limp. "Look, Foster. I don't mean to give you a hard time, but you know how it is."

"Yeah, I know it," I said, and held back a sneer. At least, I thought I held it back.

"Peepers," Samuels said and stood up.

"Yeah," McEvoy said, dropping a heavy hand on my shoulder. "Peepers."

"Here's a little advice, Foster. Don't find any more bodies in Harbor City."

I smiled.

Samuels opened the door to the reception room just as the phone rang. He and McEvoy both turned back to look at me. The phone rang again.

Samuels said quietly, "Well, aren't you going to answer it?"

TWENTY-FIVE

We all looked at the phone. I let it ring one more time, and picked up. "Foster."

"Foster, you bastard, you're a real pain, you know that?" It was Pauly Fisher at the *Chronicle*.

"Some people were just reminding me of that."

"I don't have anything for you on any other murders yet, but I found out who buried the story about the Jane Doe."

"Yes," I said, noncommittal. I looked up at the officers. Sturgeon was standing behind them, and all three of them were watching me. I gestured that it was nothing and that they should go, which worked about as well as I could have expected. I turned away in my seat a little, so that I wasn't facing them. "Go on."

"You okay, Foster?" Fisher said on the phone. "You don't sound like your usual self."

"I'm fine," I said.

"You're not alone, is that it?" Fisher's voice lowered as though the people in my office could hear him.

"That's right."

"Okay," he said. "I'll keep it quick. That article you mentioned was by Ronald Dupree, a guy I've known for a thousand years. So I called Ron and asked him why the story had been buried. He was cagey at first, but I pushed and finally Ron told me the story was quashed by none other than Daniel Merton."

I turned farther in my seat, so I was facing the grimy window behind my desk, the cord of the phone dangling over my shoulder.

"You there, Foster?" Fisher said.

"Did your friend have any idea why?"

"No. And after he told me, he tried to make out like it was just a rumor, and there was probably nothing to it. Which tells me it's the truth."

Someone cleared his throat behind me. "Yeah," I said. "Listen, thanks. I mean it."

"Like hell you do," Fisher said. "We'll talk later when you can talk." He hung up.

That was the second time that Daniel Merton's name had come up, first with the horse and now this. Why would the head of one of the studios, one of the richest men in California, want to keep the murder of an unidentified woman in Harbor City quiet?

I turned back and cradled the phone. "My dry cleaner. My other suit is ready."

"Cut the comedy, Foster."

"All right, it was my guy at the *Chronicle*. I'd asked him to look for more murders that matched the pattern, and he was calling to say he hadn't found any." I looked Samuels in the eye. "That's the truth. Now if you boys wouldn't mind clearing out, I have some real work to do." I opened one of my desk drawers as though I were looking for a file.

"If I find out that you made my job harder," Samuels

said, "I'm going to come down on you with everything I've got."

"Doesn't look like you've got too much," I said, "if you can waste your time hanging around a peeper's office, listening to his phone calls."

Samuels tapped a forefinger against my desk. "If your friend calls you with anything," he said, "you call me with it. Otherwise, you stay away from my case."

He stalked out of the office, leaving the door open behind him.

McEvoy tipped his hat to me with one finger, nodded at Sturgeon, and then walked out. He pulled the door shut.

Like Gilplaine before them, they were telling me too much. They were telling me they didn't want this case solved by me or anybody, that there was something to hide. That was okay with me, it could stay hidden for all I cared, only there was the matter of a broken movie star and whether my word was worth a damn thing.

I looked at Sturgeon. "You, too," I said.

He raised his shoulders and pushed out his chest. "Now, look here, Foster. I'm prepared to pay you a lot of money—"

"That tune again," I said, standing up. "You can't decide if you're sticking me up or bribing me." I grabbed the edge of the door, preparing to close it. "Besides, you heard the detective, I'm not allowed anywhere near this case."

"Now, see here," Sturgeon said, "he has no right—"

"Neither do you," I said, and I shoved him gently with the heel of my hand. When he'd cleared the threshold, I swung the door closed. I stayed close, listening, waiting for him to leave. There was no sound at first. He just stood there, trying to decide what to do. Then after another minute came the sound of his footsteps crossing the floor, followed by the outer door opening and closing. I listened for his steps in the hall to be sure he hadn't doubled back. They were faint and grew fainter.

That should have been the end of it. There was nothing that made staying in it make any sense. But there was nothing about any of it that made any sense. And even telling myself that Chloë Rose had been out of her mind when I had seen her last, and heavily sedated to boot, did nothing to quiet my conscience. My word was my word, and I'd given it.

I went to the safe and got out the envelope with the check in it that Al Knox had given me the day before, and put it in my pocket, still sealed. Then I stepped into the waiting room, and locked the office behind me.

Downstairs I got my car out of the garage and took it around the block, watching my rearview to make sure that neither Samuels nor Sturgeon meant to follow me. No car stayed with me the whole way, so I completed my loop out onto Hollywood Boulevard, and started for Daniel Merton's movie studio.

TWENTY-SIX

The kid at the gate wasn't Jerry, but it might as well have been.

"I'm sorry, sir, your name is not on the list," he said, holding up his clipboard. "You're going to have to go through the gate and turn around and come back out again. There are people behind you."

I put on my most charming smile for him. "I was hired two days ago by Al Knox. You know Al Knox?"

The kid nodded. "He's my boss."

"Well, why don't you call Al, and tell him I'm here. Dennis Foster. He'll tell you to let me through."

Somebody behind me let go with their horn and held it down. I checked my rearview. There was a black coupe behind me and a truck behind that. It was the truck driver who was honking.

The noise startled the kid, who ducked back into the box and picked up a phone. He came out a moment later.

"I'm sorry, Mr. Foster," the kid said, back at my window. "Mr. Knox wasn't in the office just now."

"Well, did you ask anyone else if they knew me? I was just here the day before yesterday."

The truck horn had not let up.

"Look, call the office back, tell them I'm coming in, and open the gate before that truck driver ruins the soundtrack on all of the pictures being made."

"I don't think I can do that, sir."

"I think you can. Just step back inside and try."

He blinked, looked back at the truck driver, and waved his hand. "Would you quit it?" The horn kept blaring. The kid looked all around again and shook his head. "I'm sorry, sir. You'll have to come around."

He hit the button that made the bar go up and then stepped in front of my car, guiding me, forcing me to turn around unless I wanted to hit him. From the other side of the booth, he triggered the exit gate, and I pulled back out onto Cabarello Boulevard.

The studio wall continued along Cabarello until the next intersection, where it turned right, maintaining the perimeter. I followed it until the next opening, a smaller gate just large enough to be used by one vehicle at a time. There were large wrought-iron gates that opened inward and would be shut at night. A heavy chain was suspended across the opening with a sign hanging from the middle that said, "Private. No Trespassing." The security officer here was an older man with a soft belly, no doubt one of Knox's retirees. I pulled up to the gate as another car was turned away.

"Any chance of getting in here today?" I said.

"About as good a chance as any other day," he said.

"I should be expected."

"Believe me, they all should be expected. You got a screen test with DeMille or Hughes or some other director that doesn't even work at our studio but across town at the competitor's? Or are you good friends with Chet Gelding or John Stark, or maybe it was Layla Carlton?"

"Al Knox hired me a couple days back to work a private

investigation. I'm just trying to get in to see him, but the boy at the front gate couldn't get Al on the phone."

"Where do they find these kids?"

"Will you at least call Al?"

"You a cop?"

"Not anymore."

He nodded. "What's your name?"

"Foster. And if you don't get Knox, I actually *am* friends with John Stark," I said, and smiled.

"You can leave that one in your hip pocket. I'll get Knox. Just a matter of knowing where to reach him. Hang on."

He went over to the side of the gate, opened a little panel there and brought out a phone receiver. He talked a few moments, waited, talked a bit more, then hung up and closed the little panel. He unclipped the side of the chain nearest him, and walked it across the opening, clearing the path through the gate. He waved me on. As I pulled up, I said, "Thanks."

"I guess it was about time for my daily exercise anyway," he said.

I pulled in to the studio. Security wasn't as useless as Knox had made it out to be. It might not have been impossible for a strange man to appear on the set of one of their movies, but it would take a little doing.

I followed the streets as best I could coming from the side entrance. I passed through the shadow of two soundstages and arrived at the four-story administrative building with the parking lot out front. I took a spot between what appeared to be an Army truck and what was for sure a Rolls Royce. I wasn't too concerned about whether Knox was available or not; I hadn't come to see him. Still, it was his house. I crossed the parking lot to the door on the end of the building with chicken wire glass, where three security golf carts were parked.

The officer on secretary duty today looked up as I came in. "Mr. Knox just got back in the office. I'm sorry about Billy. He's just doing his job."

"Aren't we all?" I said, and continued past him and on into Al's office.

He was on the phone. "No, damn it. This has nothing to do with my department or anybody else at the studio. It was an unfortunate but unrelated event." He gritted his teeth and shook his head at me. "There will be express instructions as always to allow no member of the press on the lot. And you're not to bother any of our actors either. You say whatever you damn please, but we'll sue you for slander if you get a word of it wrong." He slammed the phone and a ghost of a ring hung in the air between us.

"Dennis, what are you here for?" Knox said. His cheeks were red, and perspiration made his forehead shiny. He took out a handkerchief and wiped his mouth and then put it back in his pocket. "I don't have time for anything but business. This Ehrhardt–Rose thing is a twister just waiting to happen."

"Fine with me," I said. I pulled out the envelope and tossed it on his desk, much the way he'd tossed it on mine the day before.

He looked at the envelope. Then he reached for it, his eyes searching for an answer in mine. "What's this?"

"Something you left in my office. I'm returning it."

He puffed out his upper lip and looked up at me. "You

know, sending Rose to the nut house was a fine idea you had there. Now *everyone* thinks she killed Mandy."

"No they don't," I said.

"All right, no they don't." He held up the envelope. "You really should keep this. It would make me feel more comfortable."

"Who asked you to hire me?"

"I hired you, what do you mean? Look, I don't have time—"

"Then don't waste it repeating yourself. Who asked you to hire me? It wasn't your idea. I've seen Sturgeon in action, it wasn't his. All I want to know is, who wanted me—or some other sap like me—following Chloë Rose around?"

"Dennis…"

"I don't get paid off. I get paid to do a job. And I definitely don't get paid off when I don't even know who's paying me off and what they're paying me off for. I got hired to do a job. I didn't do it. So I don't get paid."

Knox's face sagged. "I was doing you a favor, goddamn it," he said. "I was throwing a bone your way. Why the hell couldn't you just take it and chew on it?"

"Because I'm not a lapdog, Knox. I don't fetch, I don't heel, and I don't roll over."

We stared at each other then. Taxidermied deer couldn't have done it better. Knox tapped the unopened envelope on his desk. Someone in another part of the office yelled, but I couldn't make out what it was about. Outside, the whole engine of Merton Stein Productions chugged away. Take an actress, an actor, and one of those scripts they were forever carrying back and forth out there. Slap some film in the camera. Plug in some lights, pay a violinist or two to add background melodies, and presto, you've got yourself a product you can show at theaters around the country, or drive-ins if it isn't good enough for the indoor crowd. Then do it again. Fifty times a year. A hundred. No slowdowns along the line. One part in the machinery is broken? Get another. Mr. and Mrs. America need their Sunday double feature, otherwise it would be nothing but newsreels, and we need morale to be high. Leave your dime at the door.

Knox set the envelope down. "Mr. Merton gave me the order personally. He said I should hire someone who could do a simple job, and I picked you. Okey, you bastard?"

I nodded. "Okey."

"You're not surprised."

"I can't say that I am."

He watched me. The voice down the hall yelled again, a happy sound. "I'm working with children here," Knox said.

"I'll leave you to it." I started for the door. Behind me came the sound of his chair creaking and then an exhalation as he pulled himself out of his seat.

"Now wait just a minute, Foster. Do you have something on this you want to tell me?"

"No, like I said. I got the message from you yesterday. I did a bad job. I'm fired. I even worked another case since then. Fastest P.I. in the west."

"Don't be like that, Foster. We're all acting stupid around this. Damn it, I went into this security detail so I wouldn't have to deal with this kind of thing anymore. I'm tired of blood."

I softened and leaned in toward him. "The police put me off of this thing too. Nobody wants me in it. I don't want me in it."

He waited for more. When I didn't say anything, he said, "Well, why are you here?"

"To see Mr. Merton," I said, and headed for the door.

He caught me by the shoulder. "You can't just go see Mr. Merton. You need an appointment."

"I don't think he'll make one for me, do you?"

He didn't stop me when I turned to go that time.

Merton wanted someone to follow Chloë Rose, he wanted Chloë Rose's horse, which used to be his horse, and he wanted a Jane Doe story to go away. Probably this Mandy Ehrhardt story, too. And Mr. Merton was a man who got what he wanted. So what else did Mr. Merton want? I figured I'd ask him.

The exterior walkway on the second floor cast the ground floor walk in shadow. The main entrance was a pair of double glass doors that entered into a wind block, and then another set of doors. The Merton Stein crest hung on the wood-paneled wall behind the front desk, and there were two secretaries at the desk who looked more severe than any of the security officers I'd seen so far. But I walked as though I belonged, waving and nodding to both of them, and went straight for the stairs. They might have called out after me, but I didn't wait to find out.

Upstairs, I was in another reception room almost identical to the lobby below. There was no avoiding the secretary here, a middle-aged woman with the lined face of a gorilla, her hair pulled back into a tight bun.

"May I help you?" she said. Her voice had the sand-paper rasp of a lifelong smoker.

"I'm here to see Mr. Merton," I said. I had my wallet out, already reaching for one of my cards. I held it out to her, and she looked at it without making any move to take it. Her expression did not change.

"To see Mr. Merton, you must have an appointment."

"I think if you check with him, I have an appointment."

"I make Mr. Merton's appointments," she said. She was annoyed with me, but not so annoyed that it was worth exercising a facial muscle over.

"Mr. Merton had me hired the day before yesterday. Last night—"

"I know who you are," the secretary said.

"So do I," said another voice, much friendlier, though no less stern.

I looked up. She stood in the entryway of the massive double doors just to the left of the secretary's desk. She wore a blue blouse with a red ascot tied around her neck and a tailored pair of khaki pants that ended mid-calf. Her open-toed brown heels showed that her toenails were the same color as her lips, rose red. The last time I had seen her, she had offered me those lips, and the time before that she'd been stuffing a drunk into the back seat of a car. Yeah, she was a girl that could make life very pleasant or very difficult, sometimes both at the same time.

The secretary's annoyance deepened then. "Miss Merton, I have already asked you to return home and wait for your father there." Including me she said, "Mr. Merton isn't here right now. As you know all too well, Mr. Foster, he is quite busy today handling the situation."

"That's grand, Mr. Foster, isn't it?" Miss Merton said, still from the doorway. "The 'situation,'" she mimicked.

The secretary turned white.

Miss Merton nodded her head into the mysterious dark between the doors, and said, "Come on in, Mr. Foster. We can wait for Daddy together." She passed through the doors without waiting to see if I would follow. I guess they always followed. I smiled my charming smile at the secretary and it got about the same response it had with the kid at the front gate. I walked around her desk, and let myself into Daniel Merton's office.

TWENTY-SEVEN

The lights were off and the curtains drawn, giving the room the oppressive tone of sick days in bed. Mr. Merton's desk stood by the windows, its footprint smaller than Al Knox's office downstairs, but not by much. Beside the desk there was a small school chair with attached writing surface where the stenographer would sit when Mr. Merton wanted to write something down. There was a long boardroom table off to one side with high-backed leather chairs all around it. A clutch of cozy couches in burgundy upholstery with buttons on the cushions surrounded a glass coffee table on a zebra-skin rug.

Vera Merton had chosen the couch with its back to me so that I had to walk around to the other side if we were going to talk. When I did, the shadows cut her features sharper. It didn't hurt her any. Her legs were crossed at the ankles and extended under the coffee table where I could see them through the glass. She was a lifetime of getting what she wanted when she wanted it and no realization that that wasn't true for everybody. Chloë Rose made you want to protect her. This one made you hope someone would protect you.

"There's a bar hidden away in the wall over there, if you'd like a drink." She didn't have one. In fact, it was unclear what she had been doing all alone in the dark. "I knew you were hired by my father," she said as I sat on the edge of the opposite couch.

"Only I didn't," I said, leaning forward on my thighs, my hat in my hands. "Daddy can't pay the electric bills?"

"Sometimes I like sitting in the dark. It helps me think," she said.

"And what do you think about?"

She cocked her head. "If I'm not mistaken, that was a personal question. Did you just ask me a personal question?"

"I don't know. Sometimes in my business I get personal when I'm not supposed to. Do you ask all the men that happen by to palaver in your father's office?"

"Only ones that work for my father," she said.

"So I guess around you that's all of them," I said.

"If you decide to be fresh with me, I might decide I don't like you."

"You liked me all right yesterday."

"That was yesterday."

"Well, take your time. I don't need an answer today."

She laughed at that, though it sounded as sincere as an acting class exercise. "Are you auditioning for a part? You're like a man out of my father's movies."

I smiled along with her, but said nothing.

She turned the laughter off but left the smile on. It was a perfect smile, barely a crease showing around it on her face. And it was a perfect face, a young girl's face, nineteen, maybe twenty.

"You have a knack for finding bodies, it seems," she said.

"You were there when Stark asked me to find Mr. Taylor. I didn't promise I'd find him alive."

The smile went away.

"Do you remember the question I asked you, and you told me to go ask Daddy? That's why I'm here. But Daddy's not here and you are."

"A coincidence. What was your question?"

"You're getting personal again."

"Sorry. I'll try to cut it out. What was your question?"

"What did my father hire you for?"

"Maybe that's personal," I said.

"Maybe, but you're going to tell me anyway."

"I will?"

"You wouldn't yesterday, but you will today. He hired you because of my brother, didn't he?"

"I wouldn't know," I said.

"Oh, I'm sure he told you to be cautious, he probably even had a cover story prepared for you. Was it that some crank was claiming that he had the exact same story idea as our most recent picture and that he sent it in two years ago, and now he was threatening Tommy over it?"

It was fascinating watching her guess as we sat there together in the dark. Even if she was young, she wasn't stupid; even if she was wrong, I had the feeling she might be groping in the right direction. "No," I said, "that wasn't it."

"It's got to be my brother. That's the only reason Daddy would handle something as menial as hiring a detective himself. It's the only reason he would have hired somebody instead of using someone that already worked for him."

"Sure, you're too smart for me," I said. "You knew all this days ago. You knew it before I was hired even." I nodded my chin at her. "What's with your brother that he needs a detective?"

Her confidence slipped as she realized that she might have spoken out of turn. She looked away from me, her eyes darting down and then across the distance to the blacked-out windows. "Nothing," she said. "Gambling." She looked back at me, proving that she could meet my look. "Gambling, women, too much room for blackmail." She said this last as if she didn't expect me to believe it.

I felt sorry, so I said, "I was hired on studio business. It was Al Knox, head of security who actually did the hiring. The word just came down from your father."

She didn't look relieved or placated.

"That's all I can tell you," I added.

"No, of course," she said, lifting her head up and with it her shoulders. "I try not to know anything about my father's business. When your father's a magic maker it takes all the magic out of life, because you've seen all the tricks."

"Unless he learns a new one."

She smiled, and it was her award-winning smile again. "Old dogs, Mr. Foster. Or I forget, did you say to call you Dennis?"

"I didn't say either."

She waved that away, and let her arm fall limp beside her.

"You know why I was hired. All of that business about your brother, that's just your protective side coming out."

"Let's forget about that," she said quietly. "It's in the past now."

"That doesn't always mean it goes away," I said.

Our eyes met, and I held hers. We measured our stares. One of us had to be the first to look away, and in the end I did it. I didn't want to stay any longer. "Enjoy the dark," I said, standing.

"My father's probably at the track." She didn't look up at me, but spoke straight ahead. "He's been nearly every day since the law went through. He put up the initial money to build the place before it was even legal."

"Santa Theresa or Hollywood Park?"

"Hollywood Park, of course."

"Then who runs things around here?" I said.

"Younger men," she said. Her eyes were gone.

I put on my hat and left before she had fully convinced herself that she had the right to feel sorry for herself.

TWENTY-EIGHT

In the outer office, the secretary didn't pause in her typing, even when I stood right up against her desk. "Is there a public phone around here?"

"Are you sure you don't want to just use mine?" she said in exaggerated indignation.

"No, I'm afraid the call's private."

"There's one downstairs to the right of the door."

"Thanks," I said, and tipped my hat. She never looked up.

I went downstairs and crossed the lobby to the payphone. It wasn't in a booth, just bolted to the wall. I had the operator put me through to the *Chronicle* and asked for Pauly Fisher. There was a long pause during which I watched the flags dangle listlessly on their poles, and then Fisher came on. "I've got news for you," he said.

"Give."

"I talked to a friend in the Harbor City police department, a real veteran. You talk to them down there?"

"I don't think we're friends right now."

Fisher snorted. "Well, there's at least one other case, a few years back. Same thing. Cut neck, cut thighs."

My pulse went up. "Name?"

"A Drusila Carter. She was working as a temp in a cleaning service. No record, family in the Midwest. They never even brought in a suspect."

"Anything else?" I said.

"My friend on the force said he thought he remembered the case being made a low priority. What are you onto here, Dennis? Should I be checking other parts of the city?"

"No," I said. "I just want to see things that aren't there."

"Like hell they aren't there."

"Thanks, Fisher," I said in a voice to end the conversation. Then before he could hang up: "Hey, you know anything about Merton's kids?"

He wasn't fooled by my attempt at sounding casual. "Is that what this is about, Merton's kids?"

"I don't know," I said. "Maybe."

"Well, I can't say I know much about them. Just what's in the society pages. The girl's a knockout, she's got brains, they gave her an east coast education, but she has a tendency to get lonely and to get photographed when she does. Twenty? Something like that. The boy's a few years older and there's got to be something wrong with him because for a few months he'll be all over the movie scene and then for a few months he's gone. I'd guess it's dope. All those rich kids are users."

"All right," I said. "Thanks again, and call if you get anything else."

"This better be as good a story as I think it is," Fisher said. "And you'd better not give it to anyone but me."

I made noises he could interpret however made him happy, then hung up.

I crossed the lobby to the exit. He was opening the outer door as I was opening the inner door, and I hurried two steps and slugged him on the chin with all of my one hundred and eighty pounds. It was like punching a bag of unmixed cement. Mitch stumbled backwards, holding onto the door handle to keep from falling, although he wasn't really in any danger of it until I took advantage of his momentary imbalance by throwing myself against his chest. He went down and I rushed past him out the door.

The sand-colored coupe sat at the head of the circular drive with the tall thin man at the wheel. He stood on the gas when he saw me. I ran along the building back towards the security office and my car. The Packard started without any trouble, and I was able to pull it out and make it to the first intersection before the coupe appeared in my rearview mirror.

The way I had come into the studio would require the guard to unlatch the chain again, which would take too long, so I turned left towards the main entrance, where I could ram the wooden gate if I needed to. I pushed the car as fast as I could between the soundstage buildings, causing people to jump out of the way and one car to swerve and honk furiously. The coupe stayed behind me, but gaining.

As I reached the front gate, a blue Lincoln was just pulling out. I gunned the motor, slipping under the black-and-white gate arm as it began to close. It banged off the back of my car. My front bumper bottomed out, scraping against the road as the shocks absorbed the decline to the street. I took advantage of the blocked lane of traffic trying to get into the studio and turned right onto Cabarello.

I went through one light and then a second with no sign of pursuit, and then the coupe appeared several cars back and one lane over. Either it wasn't so essential that they keep me in sight or they were confident they could catch up later. The traffic on the main thoroughfare acted as a barrier, but it also prevented me from getting away. I wove my way between the cars, changing lanes frequently, and made a sudden left turn at Underhill without signaling, earning me more angry honking.

I stepped on the gas, shifting up to third gear, and then to fourth, going much too fast in too highly populated an area. The coupe was behind me, doing the same, and it appeared to be gaining again. I pulled up the hand brake and jerked on the wheel, making a hairpin turn onto a residential street, then released the brake and flooded the engine as I sped down the block. I repeated the maneuver at the next corner, slamming my tail end into a telephone pole, almost losing control of my spin, until I managed to pull the car straight again. I was moving parallel to Underhill, still heading south, in the direction of Hollywood Park Racetrack.

I eased up on the speed, downshifting as my rearview stayed empty, and then brought it down to twenty-five, watching the mirror more than the road. When the street I was on hit California Avenue, I turned left and joined the traffic at a normal speed. It was only four blocks later that the sand-colored coupe was visible, weaving between the cars, two blocks behind me. I increased the gas, and made the turn onto Amity that would descend into the Valley, going through undeveloped rock formations before bottoming out in Hollywood Park. The winding road was clear of traffic, and I continued to increase my speed as best I could as the road switched back and forth, all the while descending.

The view behind me at first remained clear as well, but soon the sand-colored coupe would appear just before each curve, playing peek-a-boo behind the rock walls. Each turn, the coupe would stay in sight just a little bit longer, and soon they were taking one turn just as I was taking the next. We passed a produce-and-flowers shack built on a sandy lot where the space beside the road jutted out far enough. Around the next bend, there were more buildings on the left. Soon the rock wall would fall away from the right as well, and we would be back in a residential area. It would be better for me then.

But an explosive crack caused me to jerk the wheel, veering into the oncoming traffic lane, while looking behind me to find that the coupe was no more than thirty yards behind. There was another crack. Mitch was leaning out the passenger side window, trying to steady a gun as he aimed at me. Neither shot had cracked my windows, so I decided he must be aiming for my tires. I pulled onto the right side of the road, and another car flashed by, the sound of its horn dropping through the registers. As it passed the coupe, the thin man pulled into the oncoming traffic lane and gunned his car, bringing it within a few feet of my left taillight. Mitch shot again. The bullet pinged off of the body of my car. The sky grew to the right, the rock receding and houses appearing below. The sand-colored coupe's front right wheel was even with my back left wheel. I took my foot off of the gas and jerked the steering wheel hard to the left. I slid along the front seat from the impact, my bruised ribs bringing my stomach up to my throat and the taste of vomit into my mouth.

The coupe veered off to the left while its driver tried

to regain control. A red car, maybe a Chrysler, maybe a Pontiac, appeared, nosing out of a residential street ahead. The coupe slammed into it, causing the red car to spin ninety degrees, and bringing the coupe to a stop after a forty-foot skid that left a trail of burnt rubber on the pavement. I managed to maintain control of my Packard and I continued on, watching the rearview for two more blocks, unconvinced that the coupe was out of commission. But they remained where their car had stopped.

I wondered if it had been Knox or Merton's secretary who had called them in, or if maybe I had been followed this morning without noticing after all, but in the end I decided it didn't matter.

There was a siren already in the air. I put all my weight down on the gas pedal.

The racetrack was only another ten minutes away.

TWENTY-NINE

The Hollywood Park Racetrack was on a large stretch of land south of Hollywood that had been fields five years before. The parking lot was a patch of dirt outside of the grandstand, a three-story high, shingled edifice painted white. It shone in the California sun and blocked the view of the track from the lot. People had been opposed to the legalization of horse racing in the state, afraid that it would bring with it organized crime, more alcoholics, and debt-ridden gamblers. They were right; it had brought those things. But the main investors in the track had not been gangsters. They were the Hollywood brass. The head of just about every studio had put money into the Hollywood races, and they came to watch as often as possible.

Inside the grandstand was a crowd of men who had nowhere else to be in the middle of a weekday afternoon. They lined up nine and ten deep at the twelve brass-barred windows where tellers took the money eagerly pushed through the bars and handed back slips of paper. Drifts of spent papers littered the floor, kicked and crumpled underfoot, ignored. There were large windows looking down into the horses' stables so you could get a good look at the contenders. A large mechanical letter board of the kind used in train stations took up part of an enormous wall to the right of the tellers' windows. It rattled through the names of horses, showing that day's previous races in first, place, and show, with spots for the upcoming races left blank. Most of today's races were already finished. Another board beside it showed the names of the horses in the next race and the odds. A chalkboard with the same information was posted in the tellers' room, kept up to date by a small man in a gray suit. Ceiling fans worked at stirring the air overhead.

I looked at the harried tellers behind the counter, and took one step in their direction. I got dirty looks from no less than three of the marks, who didn't want anyone getting in the way of their emptying their wallets. I turned and went the other direction, through one of the large open archways that led out into the stands. There was a lot of well-tended dirt in an oval around a lot of well-tended grass. The starting gates were being rolled into place. Several horses carrying bright-colored jockeys were stamping the track behind the gates. An amplified voice kept up a running commentary, listing the names of horses and the names of jockeys, goading people into placing bets. The grandstand was just under half full, the crowd thick down near the track and then spread out all along the upper seats. Above that, there were large windows open to the air. The V.I.P. section. I went back inside.

A white-haired Negro custodian in a blue uniform shirt and matching pants was using a rake to gather up the slips of paper on the edge of the crowd. He had a garbage can on wheels just behind him. He was unconcerned by the frenzy, and showed no resentment when a mark walked through his carefully collected pile. I pulled out a five as I approached, but then a second mark kicked through the

Negro's work and I switched it to a ten. I held it down near where his hands were on the rake so he would see it. He stopped scraping and looked up, causing creases to form in stacks on his forehead.

"Now I know you know I don't take bets, officer," the Negro said.

I didn't correct him. "Show me where the V.I.P.s sit, the owners, the studio brass. Upstairs, right?"

He turned his eye to my outstretched hand, still holding the ten, still without taking it. "The stairs are right over there," he nodded. "I know that's not worth ten." He looked back up at me again, waiting for me to say what it was I wanted.

"I need in. I was told Daniel Merton was here. I need to see him. Is that enough?"

He nodded his head and took the bill. "You'll need another one of those for the boy upstairs," he said.

I nodded. He led the way across the room. A race had started and the space around the teller booths was nearly empty. The door to the stairs was underneath the big board. It was a narrow steep set of wooden stairs that were painted green. The heat was bottled up inside and I began to sweat before we'd even climbed halfway. "You ever find a winning ticket in all of that mess?" I asked him.

"I never have," he said without turning around.

There was another door at the top of the steps under a naked light bulb. He went through, holding the door for me. We were in a kind of vestibule open to the air on both sides. I could tell by the sound that the race was already over. He went and talked to an identically dressed young Negro standing guard outside a set of double doors opposite the door we'd come through. The youth looked at me and then back at the old man and shook his head. The old man said something more and the youth shook his head again. I walked up. "What's the problem?"

"Damn fool don't know where his mouth is to feed it," the old Negro said.

The youth turned to me. "I can't let anyone through these doors that's not a founder. There's no way to get in other than past me. I'd lose my job. What sense does that make, old man?"

I reached into my pocket and brought out another ten, my card, and a pencil. I turned the card over and wrote three names on the back. I held the ten and the card out to the youth. "Take this to Daniel Merton. Tell him I'm outside and that I'd like to talk to him. He'll tell you to let me through."

The youth looked at the ten and looked again at the old man. Then he took the money and the card. "Don't let anyone past," he said, and slipped through the door, which closed behind him.

"Kids today," the old man said, and headed off through the door to the stairs.

The echoing voice of the announcer continued its pitch. Better keep the patrons' anxiety running high, right up to the last race. It was near on dusk now and the track would be shutting down soon. Then all of the winners and losers would cross to the strip of bars across the street, whether in celebration or to drown their defeat.

The door opened and the young Negro gestured me inside. "It's the last one," he said stepping past me. He closed the door without even looking back.

It was a long narrow hallway with painted green doors every five to twenty feet. A brass number marked each door starting at one. There was no way to tell if any of the other boxes were occupied. I figured they were probably filled about as much as the grandstand, just below half. There was an unpainted door in the middle of the hall with no number that must have been the janitor's closet. The last door was numbered fifteen and it had been left open.

It was a small booth. Just four chairs along the short wall at the front. The entire track could be taken in at one glance. There were telephone extensions on both sides of the booth at seat level for calling in bets. Merton was alone. He sat in the chair all the way to the left. He didn't turn around.

I stepped between the two chairs on the right so that he could see me.

"Have a seat," he said, still without looking at me.

I left a seat between us. In profile he looked like a Roman emperor on an ancient coin. He wore a dark three-piece suit with a starched white shirt. The shadows were deep enough that I couldn't see very much of him. The family clearly had a predilection for sitting in the dark.

He didn't say anything. Neither did I. The announcer's quick patter announced that the last race of the day was about to begin. The horses were already at their starting gates. There was a moment of anticipation and then the sound of a pistol and the announcer cried, "They're off." His voice then droned like a dentist's drill, telling us what we were seeing. Merton kept his eye on the race but with an expression of indifference. I couldn't tell if he had bet on it. The horses pounded around to the far side of the track, turning into miniatures. Then they came back around the bend, the clatter of their hooves only just audible over the crowd and the announcer. A red jockey and a green jockey were out a length ahead of the pack, which was bunched close enough that show could have gone to any of them. They barreled past where the gate had been. The red jockey eased his horse out ahead of the green one and they came into the finish that way, the third horse still half a length behind. The people in the grandstand started filing back towards the doors. There was a sense of deflation in the announcer's voice.

Merton spoke then. It was the measured voice of a powerful man who had not yet decided to use his power. "What do you want?"

"Your boys followed me from the studio, but they didn't quite do their job, did they?"

"Hub's boys. Hub gets overexcited sometimes."

"Well, when his instructions are to put a stop to all unnecessary inquiries, I could see how he might get confused."

He ignored that, and said again, "What do you want?"

"To not be played for a fool, first off," I said.

"You are not a fool. Al Knox made a mistake there."

"Did he say I was?"

"No. I couldn't imagine that he would know anyone who wasn't."

"You should try sitting down in the stands sometime, then maybe you wouldn't be so surprised by what the rest of us are like."

Merton held up a hand, his five fingers spread to silence me. "What do you want?"

"Well, since I found you where your daughter told me you'd be…" That got me nothing. "…I guess I want to talk to your son."

"That's not possible."

"Do I work for you or do I work for the studio?"

"That's the same thing."

"No, it isn't. Not when I go to the cops with everything I've got. I've left some of it out until now, but I can't do that forever, and I need to know which parts need to be told which way."

"Just the other day I read a story in the paper," he said. "I thought at first I'd try to make a picture out of it, something mysterious and catchy." He held his outstretched hands in front of him, framing an invisible marquee. *The Great Unknown.*" He paused a moment and then dropped his hands. "Then I saw there's no commercial appeal. But the story still grabs me."

"I think it would be best if I talked to your son before talking to the police or the press—"

He went on talking over me. "Apparently there are people living in South America in the middle of the jungle who have never seen a white man. These people still live in a pre-literate, prehistoric state. They hunt, and they gather their food. They wear almost no clothing. They live like our ancestors did thousands of years before us. They don't know we exist."

"Then how do we know they exist?" I said.

"Stories told by other tribes. Careful anthropologists. They exist," Merton said. "I don't doubt that." He glanced at me for the first time, but my face must have been just as hidden by shadows as his was to me. "These people have never seen a movie. They don't even know that movies exist. They don't know that cameras and film exist. They don't know that artificial light exists. They can't even imagine them since they have no frame of reference. No guns, no airplanes, no cars. We know these people exist, but for them, *we* don't exist." He paused, stilled by his own revelation. When he spoke again, it was with unguarded wonder. "Should we contact these people?" he said. "Are they better off knowing less? Without our wars and our diseases and our entertainment?"

"I don't know about them, but from where I'm sitting, sometimes I think it would be nice if this city didn't exist."

"If no one knows about something," he said, "then it doesn't."

I saw where he was going then. "But I know. I know you wanted someone to take the fall for Chloë Rose's murder. Only she wasn't the one who got murdered, Mandy Ehrhardt did. But I'm not going to take the fall for that one either. Not when it's your son that killed her, and at least two other girls that you covered up for him. Now, Mr. Merton, I need to speak to your son."

His voice was measured, calm, dispassionate. "We never thought you'd really take the fall if Chloë was killed. Hell, we didn't want Chloë to be killed, she makes too much money for the studio. But if it happened—if your presence didn't prevent it—you'd have provided some cover. Some delay."

"That's what you say now," I told him. "If it had been more convenient to make it stick to me, you'd have done it.

Circumstantial doesn't mean a thing in this town if the right people are involved."

He waved his hand in a noncommittal way.

I stood. "I think I'll see the police now."

He dropped his hand and spoke without tearing his gaze from the empty racetrack. "1313 West Market Place in Harbor City," he said. "Too many people have been paid off over this; too many people who want to protect themselves. You were just insurance."

I nodded, but he couldn't see me. "That's fine. I just need to make sure I'm protected too." I pulled open the door, and then stopped. "Why'd you want to buy the horse back?"

"I love that horse," he said, matter-of-factly. "I couldn't let it go to that idiot Rosenkrantz if Chloë were to die."

I had nothing to say to that.

"My boy won't talk to you," Merton said.

I left the room.

THIRTY

I stopped at a bank of payphones and put a call through to Samuels at the Harbor City station. I checked the time. Nearly 6:30.

The officer who'd answered came back on the line after setting the phone down for long enough that I'd had to deposit another nickel. "The detective's not here."

"Is he working tonight or did he already go home?" I said.

That earned a sigh. "Mister, I'm not in charge of where everybody is around here. I'm not even in charge of where I am around here. I just answer the phone."

"Will you take a message or is somebody else in charge of that?"

"You know how many years I had to train to answer this phone? Two years, and that's not counting kindergarten. And you know how many years I've had to answer this phone? Five years, and that's a quarter of the way to my pension. So you want to tell me what it is you've got to report or can I go back to waiting for some other slob to make the thing ring?"

"How many years did you train to talk like that?"

"Ah, go to hell."

"What's Samuels' home number? Maybe I can get him there."

"Mister, I'm going to hang up now."

"Hang on," I said. "Here's the message. Tell Samuels that Dennis Foster called. Tell him to meet me at 1313 West Market in an hour." I looked at my watch again. "Make that an hour and a half. Tell him it's important. You got that?"

"I got it. An hour and a half. 1313 West Market. Shake a leg. It's beautiful. It's a poem."

"It's a message, and he'd better get it."

"I get it, it's a message. Maybe someday someone'll take a message for me."

"A man can dream."

He hung up.

I went to my car and was out on the road in under a minute. It was downhill from Hollywood Park almost the entire way, and I had to keep reminding myself to lay off the gas a little. A minute would go by and I would remind myself again. The closer I got, the more I started to feel that something was not right. Merton had not acted defeated when he gave me the address. There was something I was missing. I noticed my speedometer again and eased off.

The neighborhood wasn't about to be written up in any magazines. These were rows of small houses, each one only slightly larger than a shotgun shack. Many of them were unpainted, hard to see in the dark. The bathmat of grass in front of most of the houses was bordered with chain link fencing. I watched the stenciled numbers on the curb to find which one was 1313. It was painted at least, white, and caught whatever light there was, but there were no lights inside. I pulled up to the curb halfway down the block and walked back. Families were sitting out on their front stoops, trying to get whatever relief there was to be had out in the evening air. The sound of children playing in the dark came to me softly from the end of the street. I kept my eyes forward and my head down.

Some of the shingles at 1313 showed the wood through in the centers and some were replacements, unpainted altogether. The lawn had been hacked at without achieving a positive effect. The push mower leaned beside the front stoop. I mounted the three steps and knocked on the wooden edge of the screen door. No answer. No lights. No sounds. I knocked again. The door rattled in its frame. The latch was off. I waited another moment, and when there was no response, I opened the screen door and tried the doorknob inside. It opened, swinging in.

Inside, the smell of alcohol was strong. I closed the door behind me and listened for any sounds. Still nothing. I found a switch by the door and turned the overhead light on. It was one large room with an open door at the other end that led to a kitchen. The floor was bare wood without a rug. The living room furniture consisted of a couch and matching armchairs upholstered in peach-colored leather. It had been expensive when it was bought, but the years had worn away the stain in the places people would sit, and there was a ragged gash in the back of one of the armchairs. There wasn't any other furniture and I figured the couch for a convertible. The rest of the floor was strewn with clothes and trash with no attempt to separate the two. It was the sign of a most slovenly bachelor.

He was sitting in the other armchair, facing the door. His clothing was not at all slovenly, but instead an expensive tailored blue suit of the kind that was necessary if your friends were of a certain caliber. The coat was draped over the back of the chair behind him. That left him in a monogrammed off-white shirt with the sleeves rolled up. The monogram was TOM. He had thick dark hair that he wore pushed back from his forehead. He might have had something nice he called a face, but his head was hanging down at an awkward angle, hiding his features. He could have been asleep or passed out or maybe nodded out on morphine if it wasn't for the blood. His wrists had been cut lengthwise along the veins, and the blood had stained the arms of the chair and dripped in long strands down the sides. There was no knife in his hand, but there were a couple of empty liquor bottles at his feet. Judging by the smell, most of the alcohol had gone into the floorboards and not into Thomas Oliver Merton.

I crossed to the couch, not touching anything. I bent down and looked under the couch and chairs to see if the knife he had used was anywhere to be found. What I found instead was two glasses, one by the leg of the couch the other near Merton's feet. The glass by the couch still contained two fingers of what smelled like bourbon. The glass at Tommy's feet was nearly emptied. There was a hypodermic needle. There was no knife.

My mind went over it even as my thighs complained about squatting so long. The police wouldn't trust a suicide without a weapon nearby, it was always hard to believe the dead man had gotten up to put it away before he died. The scene could play suicide or homicide, depending on which facts the police were convinced to ignore. The hypodermic could be the last ounce of courage to go through the business with the wrists or it could be an overdose to make it easy for someone else to make the cuts. Merton Senior must have known that his son was dead when I saw him at the races. He wanted it to go murder to avoid the scandal of suicide in the family. He'd played me for a fool again when he'd given me the address. If a recently hired private dick was found at the scene, it was good for the murder rap. The police would be there any moment, no doubt. But Merton hadn't counted on me calling my own police too. That hurt his frame and meant the police would like someone else for the murder. Suicide would be better for everyone.

I stood and crossed back to the door and killed the light. Lights from other houses on the street provided a weak orange glow through the windows. I gave my eyes a moment to adjust and then made my way back to the couch. I took out my handkerchief and picked up both glasses. It was better for the police to think that Tommy had been alone, and two glasses would put someone else in the room, at least at some point in recent memory. I went into the kitchen and dumped their contents in the sink and then set the glasses in the basin. There were other unwashed dishes there. No one would notice a couple more. Tommy Merton hadn't been big on cleanliness.

I got out my penlight and started going through drawers. The drawer closest to the back door was a junk drawer, filled with unmatched buttons, broken springs, a screwdriver and a hammer, matchbooks, string, the kind of things people kept around just in case. The three drawers below it were empty. The house was clearly just a place for when Tommy couldn't make it home or to his father's office, or maybe when he wasn't welcome at either. Maybe he didn't have any silverware besides what was in the sink.

I crossed to the set of drawers on the other side of the sink, between the stove and the icebox. There was loose silverware in the top drawer, but nothing sharper than a butter knife. The next one down had the carving knives. I picked a knife that wasn't long enough to be unwieldy, but was sharp enough to do real damage. It could have been the knife. There wasn't any reason to say it wasn't. Except if the knife was wrong the M.E. would know, because one knife doesn't cut the same as another. But I had the feeling the M.E. wouldn't be as diligent as he normally was. The police like a neat suicide to keep their murder rate down, and there might be somebody exerting pressure to not look a gift horse in the mouth. I held the knife handle through my handkerchief and shut the drawer.

Before I could take a step, the front door opened and closed with a click. There was the sound of the switch and then the light in the front room went on, spilling a rectangle onto the kitchen floor.

THIRTY-ONE

I stood still and listened. There was no audible reaction to the sight of the dead man. The police would have knocked first and there would have been at least two of them, but no one spoke. Footsteps crossed the floor and stopped right about where Merton's body was. They were high-heeled footsteps.

I stepped into the doorway. Vera Merton was standing in front of her brother. She was wearing the same clothing I had seen her in that afternoon. She reached into a small clutch purse, her head down, her hair hiding her face. When her right hand withdrew from the bag it was holding a silver-plated .22.

"You won't need that. He's already dead," I said, stepping into the room.

Her head jerked up. Her eyes were red despite an expert attempt to hide the signs of crying with makeup. The hand with the gun in it jerked up too, drawing a bead on my chest.

"And you might want to turn out the light. Anyone can see you from the street through that window."

She didn't look behind her to see which window I meant. She steadied the gun. "What are you doing with that knife," she said.

I reversed my hold on the knife so that it was not threatening. "Knife's missing from the scene. I was just going to add it in. It'll look more real that way. You really don't need the gun."

She didn't lower it. "What are you doing here?"

"Your father sent me. I think he meant for me to take the fall for this."

Her face broke a little then, and no makeup could hide the pain in it. "He called me and said that he was going to call the police. I was just going to make sure…I knew Tommy was…"

"I'm taking care of it. Put away the gun and turn out the light. We haven't much time."

She lowered the weapon then, but she didn't move. Instead her eyes went back to the body, and her head and shoulders fell. She might have been crying.

I went and turned out the light. "How'd your father know what was here?"

"He came by this afternoon."

"Your brother gets a lot of visitors for a dead man."

I stepped around her, wiped the knife clean with my handkerchief, pressed it against his fingers, and then put it on the floor below his hand.

She spoke behind me. "Father wanted to talk about Tommy's options. As if Tommy had any options."

I checked the window. There was no sign of the police. Even with the lights out, we could probably be seen from outside. I took her arm. "We have to go. Where'd you park your car?"

She didn't move. "There's something wrong with us, isn't there?"

"Nothing a little hard work wouldn't cure."

She looked up then, her eyes hidden in the dark. "Hard

work!" There was a note of hysteria. "Do you know what Tommy did? What we let him do again and again?"

I took the gun out of one hand and her purse out of the other. I put the gun back where it had come from and held onto both. "Yes. I saw his work yesterday and it was much worse than this."

She looked back at her brother. "He had no more options."

"Maybe he did and maybe he didn't. Maybe he would have gone to the police or gotten some help. Maybe he would have snapped out of it. It doesn't matter. He has no options now."

"I had no more options. And now…"

"Don't say it. Don't say anything else. I'm working for your father, so I'm helping you out of a jam, but if I were to know otherwise we'd have to have some law in it. You understand?"

She nodded her head.

I checked the window again and saw a black-and-white parking silently across the street. I pulled her arm again. "Come on. We're out of time."

There was the sound of car doors slamming. She was pliant now, and I dragged her into the kitchen, her high heels clicking on the floor behind me. When the police walked in, they would see a poor slob who had written his own ticket. Merton could fix anything else that needed fixing himself. Except for Mandy Ehrhardt. She had been a cold one, but that didn't change what happened to her. It was better that Tommy got his own.

We went out the back door in the kitchen. I pushed her ahead of me and closed the door behind us. The backyard was a slab of concrete with overflowing metal garbage cans tucked up against the house. A small chain fence enclosed the slab with an opening that let into an alley. When they got no answer, one of the cops would come back here. I wanted to be out of the alley before then.

I hurried us down the narrow path between the slabs of concrete. There were fences all the way, creating a wall that separated people's private garbage from the public trash. "Where's your car?" I asked again.

"I parked on Front Street, one block over." There were no tears in her voice now, and some of her self-assurance had returned.

I let go of her arm and she stayed with me. "Good. Go to your car and get out of here."

"What are you going to do?"

"Does it matter?"

She didn't answer. We were at the end of the alley now, stepping onto the adjoining street. She took her purse from me, and left without a word. I went the opposite way to come back around to West Market. I crossed the street and hurried along to my car. If I were just getting here, I would be coming from my car.

THIRTY-TWO

Both uniforms were still at the door. Or maybe they had already checked the rear and had come back around to the front. They pounded on the door again, loud enough that I could hear them halfway down the street. The summer night sounds of the neighborhood had died away, killed by the police cruiser.

Once they went inside, I could pull away. But before I could get in my battered Packard, an obvious unmarked pulled up and double-parked along the marked car. I waited a moment and then started up the middle of the street for it. Samuels got out. He was by himself. He saw me coming and said as I reached him, "You call the law?"

"No," I said. "Just you."

"What's going on?"

"I think this guy is your man. Other than that I don't know any more than you do."

Samuels led the way up the walk. We were friends again. "Officers," he said to the other cops, "Detective Samuels with Robbery/Homicide. What's the trouble?"

"Call about a possible prowler. Nobody's home."

I liked the call about the prowler as much as I liked having my teeth kicked in.

"Step aside," Samuels said, and stepped between them and banged on the door with his fist. He turned back to me, still standing on the path. "How sure are you about this?"

"Sure," I said.

"We'll get a warrant later," Samuels said, and opened the screen door and tried the knob, which opened for him as well as it had for me. He stepped inside and the lights came on. The officers followed after him, and I followed behind. The scene was just as stunning the second time. "Damn it!" Samuels said. He turned on me. "Okey, spill. Wait a second." He turned to the officers. "This was your call. You call it in, and wait outside for the dusters to get here." Once the two policemen, one ashen faced, the other red, were gone, Samuels turned on me again. "That's Daniel Merton's kid. You going to tell me something now?"

"Remember the other case, the one before Christmas? Merton had the story quashed. There's another one a couple years back. Merton probably killed that one too, because it never went anywhere. When I looked into it, a couple of Hub Gilplaine's stooges used me for a punching bag. They tried to prevent me from seeing Merton earlier today too. I'm guessing Gilplaine was blackmailing the old man, and it wasn't worth anything if other people knew. I managed to check in with the old man anyway and he gave me this address. I called you and you know the rest."

He looked at me with narrowed eyes. "I don't like it."

I shrugged and kept my mouth shut.

"You're claiming that Thomas Merton killed at least three girls and that his father has covered it up for him? Do you know who Daniel Merton is?"

"Sure," I said.

He looked back at the stiff. "I don't like it. But I guess I'll take it. What did Merton senior say when you talked to him?"

"He said that it was okay if his kid killed a couple of girls as long as nobody noticed. I guess killing a girl who's going to be in a picture gets noticed. And so we have it."

"He told you that?"

"Not in those words."

"Well, you keep a lid on this thing. We'll figure something out."

"You always do, detective," I said.

He gave me another squinty-eyed look and then dismissed the comment with a wave of his hand.

"There's more," I said.

He shook his head without even looking at me. "You're going to tell me this other stiff under the boardwalk was Merton's too."

"You're pretty good at this," I said.

"I'm also good at using my gun as a club without knocking it out of line. You want me to show you that trick too?"

"You said you like it straight."

"Like it? I don't like it one bit." He sighed. "Give it to me short. We'll go back to the station and you can tell it as long as you want."

"Tommy and Greg Taylor were friends. They were both out, looking to get high. I'm guessing Tommy killed Ehrhardt on the way. When he realized Taylor could be a witness, he took care of him also."

He looked at me. "This isn't the world we were born

into," he said. "It wasn't like this when we were kids. If a man killed you, he did it looking you in the eyes and he had a good reason, and everyone slept all night."

"You believe that?"

"Not for a second," he said, and went back outside.

I followed, leaving the door open.

THIRTY-THREE

At the station, I gave the police my story, leaving out
Daniel Merton at Detective Samuels' suggestion. I then
went home and gave the story, leaving in everything, to
Fisher. Then I collapsed on my bed. When I came to, the
sun was shining, and I went out for a newspaper in the
same clothes I had on.

There was no mention of Merton on the front page—
not the father, not the son. I took the paper back home
and read through every article, but there wasn't one on
the Mertons or on the Ehrhardt killing. I went back down
to the newsstand at the corner and bought three other
papers and took those back upstairs and read through
every article in those too. Nothing. The fix was in. That
left me a loose end.

I considered the house visits I needed to make while
deciding if I should change my clothes. In the end I left
without changing. At the studio, my name was on the list.
When I got up to the secretary's desk, she picked up her
phone at the sight of me and had it back on the receiver
by the time I was in front of her.

"You're to go right in," she said, without a hint of expression.

I went through the door. The curtains were open this
morning. It made the office feel grand and light. Merton
was at his desk with a folder open in front of him and
three more to the side. Two telephones had appeared

on the desk as well. Maybe he locked them up at night.

He looked up. His face was stern.

"Aren't you in mourning?" I asked.

"I still have to eat," he said.

We looked at each other, holding eye contact for half a minute before I decided there was nothing in it and looked away.

"I hope you know I didn't expect that murder rap to stick on you," he said.

"Sure, suicide plays just as well, and it's easier to keep it out of the papers."

"I can keep anything out of the papers I damn well want to."

"I've noticed that."

He leaned back in his chair and the bluster drained away. An old man looked back at me. "It had to stop. He was getting too hard to control."

"I've got no problem with what you did."

"Not me," he said.

And then I flashed on it. That's why she had been sitting in the dark.

"Some family you've got," I said.

"It'd make a great picture," he said. "Too bad I can't make it." Then he leaned back over the open folder. "My secretary has a check for you. I filled in an amount, but if it's wrong, she can write you another one." He turned a page in the file. I was dismissed.

The secretary gave me my check without any comment. It was for $2,500. I considered tearing it up and walking out, but that wouldn't do anybody any good. I went down to my car to make my final stop.

The Enoch White Clinic was housed in two adjoining mansions and five outbuildings that had been built by oil men in the years before the pictures came to southern California. Signs along the long drive pointed the way through the acres of grass and trees to a parking lot that had been poured in front of the eastern of the two main houses. The door displayed a brown placard with business-like letters that read RECEPTION.

The front hall was two stories high, a large bank of arched windows at the rear displaying the grounds behind the house. It was a peaceful view that suggested that the city was far away or maybe that there was no city at all. It was the kind of view that you could grow to love until it made you lonely and became stifling. The reception desk was to the right facing away from the window. I had to sign my name on a clipboard and they asked me to take a seat in one of the chairs that were provided for visitors. I was the only one there. The house was silent. They kept the crazies under wraps here. Screaming was bad for business.

When a nurse came to get me, I followed her down a wood-paneled hallway that had large gilt-framed portraits showing men in collars and robes in between every two doors. At the end of the hall, we turned into another hall just like it. Shem Rosenkrantz was leaning against a door-frame, drinking from a flask.

"I ought to kill you," he said.

The nurse looked flustered and turned and left without saying anything or pointing out which room belonged to Chloë Rose. I think I had an idea.

"The doctors say Clotilde is sick. They won't let her go. They say she's got a nervous constitution. That she may never be able to leave. They say she's a danger to herself. They know her better than I do. They know her better than she knows herself."

"It's a private clinic. You could take her out of it at any time."

He brought up the flask, but it didn't make it to his mouth. His face collapsed and a sob escaped him. "She wanted to die. She wanted to leave me."

"And you didn't give her any reason."

The anger took over again. "I was all she had and she was everything to me."

"You had a funny way of showing it."

"You don't let up, do you? The only reason I don't sock you is that you're right." He drank then. "You bastard." His eyes were red. "You can go in," he said.

I walked around him and opened the door. She was sitting in a cane rocking chair by the window, looking at the same beautiful view I had admired in the front hall. She didn't turn when I walked in. She kept her eyes forward. She rocked herself ever so slightly with her slippered foot.

I went around the bed and put myself in front of her, but she didn't look up. Her eyes were glassy, the reflection from the window casting them white. She was well drugged. They had taken a pretty French girl and put her in the movies to be in all of our dreams. Now she was tucked away in her own dreams. The life in between was nothing but infidelities, lies, heartache, and death. The solution was the same for the victim as it was for the per-petrator. She had just gotten the order reversed: cut her wrists first, and now she was getting high.

I left without speaking. Rosenkrantz was crying into his flask. At the front desk I asked for a pen. I brought out my check from Merton and I wrote it over to Chloë Rose. She must have had money in the bank, but that money would run out with no more coming in. I handed it to the nurse, and told her to credit it to Chloë Rose's account, and to make sure she wasn't taken out of there before it ran out.

Outside in the sun, I watched the gardener play with his flowerbed, cutting away dead stalks and weeds. I went to my beaten car and got in, thinking that the casualties are often bigger than could be understood. That's why the movies never made any sense. The screen's not big enough to hold everyone in it.

THE TWENTY-YEAR DEATH
Concludes in

POLICE at the FUNERAL

Turn the page for
an exciting excerpt...

I sat on the edge of the hotel bed trying to convince myself that I didn't want a drink. The argument that it had been three months since my last drink—and that had only been one Gin Rickey—and almost seven months since my last drunk wasn't very convincing. I tried the argument that I would be seeing Joe for the first time in four years, and Frank Palmer, Sr., the lawyer, and probably Great Aunt Alice too, so I should be sober when I saw them. But that was the reason I wanted a drink in the first place.

I glared at the mirror attached to the front of the bathroom door. I knew it was me only out of repeated viewing, but now, about to see my son, I saw just how broken I looked. My hair was brittle, more ash-gray than straw, and my face was lined, with crow's feet at the corners of my eyes, sunken cheeks, and broken blood vessels across the bridge of my nose. I looked worse than my father did when he died, and he was almost ten years older then than I was now.

"You don't want a drink," I said to my reflection. Then I watched as I sighed, exhaling through my nose, and my whole body sagged.

Why the hell was I back in Maryland, I asked myself, back in Calvert City?

But I knew why. It was time to pay Clotilde's private hospital again. And I owed money to Hank Auger. I owed money to Max Pearson. I owed money to Hub Gilplaine.

And those were just the big amounts, the thousands of dollars. There were all kinds of other creditors that wouldn't be too happy to know I was three thousand miles from S.A. There had to be money for me in Quinn's will. Otherwise Palmer wouldn't have called me.

The door from the hall opened in the front room. It crashed shut and Vee appeared in the mirror, framed by the square arch that separated the rooms. "Don't you just love it?" she said.

She was in a knee-length sable coat with a collar so big it hid her neck. She wasn't bad to look at normally, deep red hair, unmarked white skin, and what she was missing up top was made up down below. In the fur and heels she looked sumptuous.

"It's the wrong season for that," I said.

She came forward. "He'd been saving it."

"I hope he's planning to p—to give you more than a fancy coat."

"He's paying for the suite." She opened one side of the coat, holding the other side across her body, hiding herself. But I could see that she wasn't wearing anything underneath anyway. She slid onto the bed behind me, putting her hands on my shoulders. In the mirror, a line of pale skin cut down her front between the edges of the fur.

"He didn't wonder why you weren't staying with him?"

She faked shock, raising a hand to her mouth in the perfect oops pose. "I'm not that kind of girl," she said, and then she made herself ugly by laughing, and flopped back on the bed, her whole naked body exposed now, her arms outstretched, inviting me to cover her.

"You were just with him," I said.

"But now I want you. That was just business anyway."

I shook my head, my back still to her, although I could see her in the mirror.

She dropped her arms. "What's wrong with you?"

"I want a drink," I said.

"Then have one."

"I can't."

"Forget what the doctors say." She was losing her patience. "You'd feel a lot better if you took up drinking again instead of always whining about it. Now come here. I demand you take care of me."

I looked back at her. She should have been enticing, but she was just vulgar. "I've got to go." I stood up.

"Like hell you have to go," she said, propping herself up. "You bastard. You can't leave me like this."

"The will's being read at noon. As it is I'll probably be late. That's what we're here for in the first place, remember?"

"You pimp. I'm just here to pay for you. I should have stayed with him upstairs. At least he knows he's a john, you pimp."

"If I'm a pimp, what's that make you?"

"I know what I am, you bastard. You're the one with delusions of grandeur."

I could have said, that's not what she thought when she met me, but what would be the point? I left the room, going for the door.

She yelled after me. "You'll be lucky if I'm here when you get back."

I went out into the hall. I should have left for the lawyer's before she got back. I had heard her go through that routine more times than I could count, but it was the last thing I needed this morning. No matter how much she got, she couldn't get enough. An old man couldn't satisfy a woman like that. But when I first met her, I hadn't felt old. She'd made me feel young again, and I hadn't realized what she was until later. I wasn't any pimp, I'll say that, but a man's got to eat, and she was the only one of the two of us working.

I took the elevator downstairs to the lobby. Instead of pushing through the revolving doors to the street, I went into the hotel bar. The lights were off since enough sunlight was creeping through the Venetian blinds to strike just the right atmosphere. It took my eyes a moment to adjust. When they had, I saw that I was the only person in the bar other than the bartender, who stood leaning against his counter with his arms crossed looking as though he was angry at the stools. I went up to the bar. "Gin Rickey," I said.

He pushed himself up, grabbing a glass in the same motion. He made the drink, set it on a paper doily, and stood back as if to see what would happen.

I drank the whole thing in one go. I immediately felt lightheaded, but it was a good feeling, as though all of my tension was floating away. I twirled my finger, and said, "Another one."

The bartender stood for a moment, looking at me.

"Room 514," I said. If Vee's "friend" was paying for the room, he could afford a little tab.

The bartender brought my second drink. "Don't get many early-morning drinkers," I said, picking up the glass.

"It's a bad shift," he said.

"And let me guess. You worked last night too."

"Until two ayem."

I tipped my glass to him and took a drink. He watched me like we were in the desert and I was finishing our last canteen. I set the glass down, careful about the paper doily. "If you came into big money, I mean as much money as you can imagine, what would you do with it?"

He twisted his mouth to the side in thought. Then he said, "I'd buy my own bar."

"But this was enough money so you didn't have to work again. You could settle down anywhere, or don't settle down, travel all over."

"What would I want to leave Calvert for?"

"Get a new start. You said yourself you were miserable."

"I said it was a bad shift."

"Aren't they all bad? Every last one of them."

He put his big palms down on the bar and leaned his weight on them. "No, they're not. Are you finished with that? Do you need another?"

I waved him away. "When you're a kid, you know how you dream you'll be a college football star or a fighter pilot? How come you never dream of just being satisfied?"

"I like tending bar."

"Right." I drained the last of my drink, and felt composed, at least enough for the reading of the will, even with Joe there.

"Kids don't know anything anyway," the bartender said. "What do you do, mister?"

"Nothing anymore. I was a writer."

"Anything I would have heard of?"

"Probably not," I said.

"You need another?"

I shook my head. I had a soft buzz on, and it felt good. It felt better than it should have. "Put the tip on the tab," I said. "Whatever you think's right."

"Thanks, mister."

I shrugged. "I just came into some money."

"Well, thanks."

I waved away his gratitude. It was making me feel sick.

I walked out of the bar and pushed my way through the revolving door in the lobby onto Chase Street. The August heat and humidity had me sweating before I got to George and turned south towards downtown. Calvert hadn't changed much since Quinn and I lived here in 1920. Or was it '21? The Calvert City Bank Building over on Bright Street that now dominated the skyline hadn't been there, and there had been more streetcars instead of busses, but overall the short and stocky buildings of the business district were the same. I remembered when those buildings had seemed tall, after *Encolpius* was published and I suddenly had enough money to marry Quinn. Now Quinn was dead and *Encolpius* and all my other books were out of print and even Hollywood had thrown me out and my life would never be as good as that day here in Calvert thirty years ago.

I was one poor bastard. If I had known how much of our married life was going to be screaming at each other and trying to outdo the other with lover after lover, pill after pill, drink after drink, I would have—at least I hope… yeah, I would have called it off. Quinn knew how to make me jealous from across the room. It was only natural when I started stepping out. And there were the two miscarriages and then Quinn started bringing a bottle to bed and finishing it in the morning, so of course I did the same. It got to the point where I couldn't think without something to get me going. We tried the cure, once in New Mexico, once in upstate New York, but it didn't last long, and when we got to Paris, we didn't care anymore, it was all-out war.

And then I met Clotilde. She set Quinn off more than any of the others. And when I began to sober up for her, Quinn left me. She told me I had a kid only after the divorce had gone through. Then Clotilde and I married and we were happy for a while at least, until we went to Hollywood, or maybe it was still in France... Anyway, she got famous, with thousands of men after her, and the public had forgotten me, so who could blame me when I had a girl or two on the side? No one. But Clotilde ended up in the the madhouse, and I was broke, and I borrowed from everybody who I knew even a little, and now all I had was Vee.

As I walked and felt sorry for myself, my mood sank lower and lower, and the effect of the alcohol wasn't helping it any. How could Quinn have left me any money after all these years? Maybe Joe had asked for me to be there, but had been too ashamed to contact me directly. I was his father after all. I passed the C&O Railroad building, and turned into the Key Building where the doorman, with a big servile grin, followed me inside, skipping ahead to reach the ornate brass elevators before I did. "Good morning, sir. Where are you off to?"

"Palmer, Palmer, and Crick, to see Mr. Frank Palmer the senior," I said.

He pushed the elevator call button and then pushed it again repeatedly. "May I ask your name, sir?"

"Shem Rosenkrantz. Do I need to be announced?"

His eyes flicked over, and he smiled and waved at someone who came in behind me. "Morning, Mr. Phelps."

Mr. Phelps started right for a door that must have led to the stairs. "Sam," he said with a single nod, and disappeared through the door.

Sam beamed back even as the door shut. How could a guy like that be happy, with a job pushing buttons and kissing ass? I guess some guys have to be that way, making everyone else feel bad because they feel so goddamn good. He turned his attention back to me. "Mr...."

"Shem Rosenkrantz." The sweat was streaming down my face. The hand of the floor indicator swung counter-clockwise, counting down the elevator's progress.

Then he answered my question from before. "No need to be announced. I just like to keep track of who's in the building. For security reasons."

The elevator bell rang and the heavy doors rolled back. A man and a woman stepped off. Sam had fresh smiles. "Mr. Keating. Sally."

They smiled and nodded and hurried to the door. I started to walk around Sam to get at the elevator. He moved out of my way, nodding his head. Then he leaned into the elevator reaching around to the control panel and he hit the button for floor eight, the top floor. He gave me one last smile, and I almost told him Quinn was dead to knock that smile off his face, but I didn't. "Eighth floor," he said, and the elevator doors closed...

SONGS of INNOCENCE

by **RICHARD ALEAS**

Three years ago, detective John Blake solved a mystery that changed his life forever—and left a woman he loved dead. Now Blake is back, to investigate the apparent suicide of Dorothy Louise Burke, a beautiful college student with a double life. The secrets Blake uncovers could blow the lid off New York City's sex trade…if they don't kill him first.

Richard Aleas' first novel, LITTLE GIRL LOST, was among the most celebrated crime novels of the year, nominated for both the Edgar and Shamus Awards. *But nothing in John Blake's first case could prepare you for the shocking conclusion of his second…*

RAVES FOR SONGS OF INNOCENCE:

"An instant classic."
— The Washington Post

"The best thing Hard Case is publishing right now."
— The San Francisco Chronicle

"His powerful conclusion will drop jaws."
— Publishers Weekly

"So sharp [it'll] slice your finger as you flip the pages."
— Playboy

**Available now at your favorite bookstore.
For more information, visit
www.HardCaseCrime.com**